Deadly Lights

Kelly McWinter PI, Book 4

Jude Pittman

Print ISBNs

Amazon Print 9780228627838
Ingram Spark 9780228627784

http://bwlpublishing.ca

Dedication

To all my Kelly McWinter fans

Jude

Table of Contents

Chapter One

Kelly McWinter parked his pickup, fondly referred to as old Blue, in the garage behind Lake Country Stables. His wife Gillian had inherited the property from her father and when she married Kelly, he'd given up his cabin at Indian Creek and moved into her sprawling ranch house just outside of Fort Worth.

They both loved the ranch, everything from the white rail fence surrounding the immaculate grounds to the well-worn and comfortable swing that welcomed him to the back porch. Kelly and Gillian spent many a hot summer night sipping iced tea or cold beer and rocking contentedly in the sultry Texas evenings, and that's just what Gillian had in mind when she came through the screen door with two glasses of tea just as Kelly mounted the steps and headed for the swing.

"Hey there!" she smiled and set the tea down on the table. "Not that I'm complaining but what are you doing home in the middle of the afternoon?"

"Wel-l-l-l," Kelly drawled out the l's, "I stopped by the Hideaway and Stella made me an offer."

"Ah ha. She's at it again is she? I'll have to have a talk with that woman." Gillian's voice trailed into laughter.

Stella Davis had married Kelly's best friend three years ago, and after a rocky start, which Kelly's friend Jude Pittman told readers about in her second Kelly McWinter book, Deadly Betrayal, she and Gillian became best friends. Stella had proven a rather persistent thorn in Kelly's side with her constant queries about when he was going to tie Gillian up before someone else came along and swept her up in his saddle. It had taken another year, but Kelly finally asked Gillian to become his wife and she had happily accepted.

"Actually, I think you might like this brainstorm of hers. You remember her niece, Marcy?"

"Of course, how could I forget after what we all went through rescuing her and saving her name. Besides, I follow her career on Entertainment Tonight, and if I miss anything I get all the details from Aunty Stella every time we talk. Did you know that she's one of this year's nominees for country music's female vocalist of the year?"

Kelly chuckled. "Guess there's not much point trying to surprise you. Did Stella tell you about the crazed fan who broke into Marcy's house?"

"My God, no. She isn't hurt is she?"

"No, at least not physically. He scared the hell out of her though, and Mark is fit to be tied."

"Oh, I sense a PI project on tap."

Kelly chuckled. "You know me too well. But you might like this one a lot better than some of my other jobs."

"I'm all ears. First, tell me about Marcy's break in."

"One of her over-zealous fans climbed the wall surrounding her Nashville property, used some kind of jammer to disarm her security system, and almost made it up the stairs to Marcy's bedroom."

"Where was Mark?"

"Apparently he's part of the legal team sent over to Russia to oversee the review of documents discovered in one of those Nazi vaults in East Germany. Russia has finally agreed to let United Nations appointees work alongside their own researchers to establish provenance of the materials and Mark's part of the team. It's a huge honor, but it's a long process and Mark will be away for at least another three months. Marcy's been on her own--well, she's not alone, like any celebrity she's always got an entourage, but she doesn't have her husband."

"She must have been terrified."

"She was, and believe it or not, the only reason the intruder didn't reach Marcy's bedroom is because Stella had given her one of Lucy's puppies and the little fella set off an alarm."

"Hey Jake," Gillian looked to where Jake had his head propped against Kelly's leg. "Good breeding."

Jake lifted his nose and shook his head, before nuzzling it back down on Kelly leg."

"Yep. Marcy said the pup had his basket right behind the front stairway. The intruder came in through the French doors and he'd no sooner set foot on the front step when the dog went into a frenzy of barking that brought everyone in the house out of their rooms."

Kelly ran his hand along Jake's back and leaned close to his ears. "Hear that, boy? One of your pups grabbed that moron's pant leg and sent him sprawling ass over teakettle down the stairs. Knocked him out cold."

Gillian, who had started grinning when Kelly described the intruder's retreat down the stairs, was now laughing so hard tears streamed down her cheeks.

"I know it probably scared poor Marcy to death, but I'd give a pretty penny to have a picture of Lucy's puppy hanging on to that idiot's pant leg as he tumbled down the stairs."

Kelly paused and joined her laughter.

"So what happened?" Gillian finally drew a breath and urged him on with the story.

"Marcy's assistant Bella called nine-one-one and got the police out there pronto. They arrested the suspect, some love crazed fan named Lucas Spadina. He'd been picked up a couple of times for trespassing and been suspected in a couple of peeping Tom cases, but nothing stuck. When the cops questioned him this time he claimed Marcy invited him to stop by and see her."

Gillian scoffed. "Not damn likely."

"Yeah, but you know how it goes. The jails are overcrowded, this guy hasn't shown any propensity for violence, and of course Marcy couldn't say for sure she hadn't casually told a fan to stop and see her sometime."

"No way!"

"Of course she didn't, but like I said, it's one of those cases. He was given community service and probation, plus he's been ordered to stay away from Marcy and her property."

"Lot of good that'll do if he's determined."

"Exactly. Which is why Stella made me an offer. Seems Marcy has to travel to Los Angeles in two weeks, she's being considered for a segment of the television show Nashville, and she's got a bunch of meetings in LA. After that, as one of the nominees, she'll be attending the ACM Awards in Las Vegas."

Gillian fixed him with a blue-eyed stare, "So?"

Kelly grinned. "Marcy asked Stella to see if you and I could go with her -- as her guests of course -- stay in a suite at the Beverly Wilshire, and then accompany her to Vegas, in a studio jet."

Gillian's smile grew wider and wider.

Kelly suppressed his grin and continued. "Once we get to Vegas we'll be staying in another suite at the MGM Grand. And oh yeah, we'll have VIP tickets to the ACM awards. You interested?"

"Are you kidding me? Am I interested? You turn that down and I might just be accused of committing justifiable homicide."

"I knew I had no business teaching you to shoot this winter."

"But you aren't licensed in California or Nevada are you?"

"Nope. I told her that, but all she wants is a bodyguard to stand in for Mark and he won't settle for anyone else. Guess we made quite an impression on the big boy."

"Well of course. After all you are the best, and I don't blame Mark. I'd want you too if my life was in danger--well actually I'd want you even if it wasn't." Gillian turned in the swing and leaned into him, pressing her lips against his.

Kelly savored the long kiss before reluctantly coming up for air. "So what do you think, Gill? We never did get a chance to go on a honeymoon. First it was foaling time and then the Martin case took me all the way down to El Paso, and what with one thing and another -- your stables and my PI work, life's been crazy this past year. I think we could use a little Hollywood style R&R. What'ya say, you up for some *Vegas, baby*?"

"Oh I'm game. Beverly Hills and then Las Vegas, first class all the way, I'd have to be crazy not to jump at the chance. You bet your life I want to go, this little gal's papa didn't raise no fool."

"Good. I'll let Stella know. I'm sure you two will have lots to discuss, like what the heck we're supposed to wear to some of those parties. I don't mind a monkey suit for the awards ceremony, but I hope we're not expected to break the bank for every party she decides to attend."

"I wouldn't worry about it, Galahad." Gillian patted his arm and leaned her head against his shoulder. I have a feeling you and I will be the least important spectators at the parties. As long as we're not in beach wear it's doubtful either one of us will warrant a second glance. I'll talk to Stella and we'll get it sorted out."

"Good. That's your department. I need to stop by the Sheriff's office and have a chat with Gus. Apparently, one of their parolees skipped his check in and seems to have disappeared. They're shorthanded right now and Gus wants me to see if I can run him to ground." Kelly got up from the swing and held out his hand for Gillian.

"That's great." She came to her feet with a smile on her face. "It'll be nice to have you home for a few days."

"Suits me fine too. Especially since I have a pretty good idea where to start. It turns out our boy's from around Azle. My biker friend Fred Todd grew up there. If anyone knows what one of the home boys are up to, it'll be Fred."

"Well, I've got chores to do, so I'll let you get on with your biker chasing, and I'll take myself out to the barn." Gillian lifted her head for a kiss, and Kelly happily accommodated her.

Despite his schedule, the last year had been the happiest he could remember in a long time. He and Gillian fit like a couple of old timers who'd watched each other grow up. They'd both experienced their personal sorrows, and the highs and lows of young love and growing pains. Even though this was her first marriage, and Kelly had done some hard healing from the tragic loss of his first wife, he and Gillian seemed to be at the same place in their lives. They suited each other's lifestyles, and met each other's needs for companionship. It didn't hurt that his gentle kitten of a wife was nothing less than a full grown tiger when the two of them shut the bedroom door.

Life was good, and a trip to the west coast, hobnobbing with the movers and shakers and living the high life, was something both of them could take full advantage of. So as long as he tended to business and kept Marcy safe, it sounded like just the kind of adventure he and his newlywed bride would thoroughly enjoy.

* * *

Gillian no sooner came back in from the barn than Stella was on the phone. "Well, did he tell you?"

"He sure did and before you ask, I'm nobody's fool. You darn right's I said yes, yes, yes."

"Oh Gill, I'm so glad. Of course I'm worried to death about Marcy, but I also want to see you and Kelly get away and have some fun together. It's going to be fan-damn-tastic for y'all."

Gillian tried to get a word in, but Stella kept right on gushing.

"Now, the first thing you're gonna do is make some decisions about your wardrobe. You're a little thinner and a few inches taller than I am, but I was skinnier the year before Andrew died. We had plans to attend the Governor's ball in New Orleans that year, and I had a gown designed for me by Valentino. Naturally, I didn't go and the gown has never been worn. It'll require some adjusting, but it's a stunning emerald green mid-calf and should be just about knee length on you. You'll be a knockout."

"Stella, I can't take your Valentino. My God, it must have cost a fortune and you've never even worn it."

"No, and I'm never going to. Listen Gill, we both know Cam's a one hundred percent good ole' boy, and there's never going to come a time when he'll willingly attend anything where I need to wear a Valentino. Nope, I've been to all the fancy parties and formal balls I'm ever going to go to, and that's fine with me."

Gillian tried to protest. "Stella, you don't know that."

A sultry chuckle from the other end of the phone. "Sugar, it's fine. Really. Yes, life is quiet in Indian Creek, but that's okay. I love things the way they are. No, I never expected to be a bartender at a place like the Hideaway Bar and Barbecue, but Cam needed me and it's a good gig for now. Maybe someday I'll put my college degree to use, but I'm in no hurry. Cam's a doll, and I'd do anything for him."

"And he would for you. You know Stella, if you wanted—"

"The only thing I want is for you to get your ass over here and try on this gown. I'm thrilled at the idea it might finally be worn. I almost gave it away to the Salvation Army truck this summer but something made me hang onto it, just in case. Now it seems like there was a perfectly good reason for that. Will you come by tomorrow and try it on? At least see if it's something you'd like to wear before we do any more arguing about it?”

"Of course I will. I'm so relieved you might have something I can wear. Trust me, I've been tearing my hair out ever since Kelly announced this trip, trying to figure out how I'm going to get a dress suitable for the awards dinner without having to sell a couple of horses.”

"Oh yeah. Like you'd really do that.” Stella, who knew full well how attached Gillian was to every horse in her stables, laughed at the suggestion. "So it's settled then. See you tomorrow afternoon. How about we do lunch? I'll get Darlene to look after the noon crowd at the Hideaway and you and I can sneak back to our place. We'll have ourselves a crab caesar washed down with one of my famous Bloody Mary's.”

"How could I pass up an offer like that? I'll see you about noon.” Gillian hung up the phone and smiled to herself. Stella was one of the best friends she had in Fort Worth, and it was funny how it all came about, considering the rocky start of their early relationship when it had seemed very likely they had their caps set for the same man.

* * *

Kelly headed over to Texas B's on Belknap. Since it was early in the day the lot was empty except for a couple of bikes, one of which probably belonged to the barmaid.

Kelly pulled old Blue up next to a gleaming Chrysler parked against the back fence.

"I see you finally got her done." Kelly walked up to the owner and stuck out his hand.

"Yo, Jake!" Fred greeted his friend with the undercover name Kelly'd used when they met.

"Well, that's good Fred, but that's not my name anymore, remember?"

"Oh, yeah. Hell, I still ain't got used to the idea you were a cop all that time when I thought I was just helping a brother biker in a jam."

"Well, you were a lot of help, and if it's not pushing my luck, maybe I can hit you up for another favor."

"Cop stuff?"

"Yes, and no. I'm not with the force anymore, I'm private. I'll be honest though, I'm helping out a cop friend. You remember Augustus Graham?"

"Oh hell, yeah. Hey, I made it into the inner circle I get to call him Gus now!"

"Damn, you must be tight. He's picky about who gets to use his nickname."

"Funny how we ran into each other. Turns out we've got grandsons in the same karate school. We met up at a rank advancement ceremony not long after you took down that dirty doctor. Of course, we don't talk shop, but we took to sitting together after that and kind of rooting on the kids. Nice guy."

"The best. So maybe you won't mind giving me a lead if you've got one. You ever heard of Wade Clements? He grew up in Azle. He'd be about ten years younger than you, but I wondered if you knew the name."

"Sure I do. His older brother Neil and I used to be tight. He went into the army, I think it was in 2001, and got shipped to Afghanistan. Didn't make it back. I went to the funeral. Let's see, that would be fifteen or so years ago. He had a kid brother, must have been about six or seven. He took Neil's death really hard. Blamed the government. I never did get the whole story, wasn't there long enough, but my recollection is Neil wasn't supposed to deploy. He was set for a special forces training program, but something happened, they cancelled his training at the last minute and he shipped out. He got no special training, other than Basic. He lasted about a week before the jeep he was riding in ran over a land mine. No survivors."

"Damn, that's tough. Probably explains what's going on with Wade, though. He was arrested for hacking into the Defense Department's computers. It was a first offense and his lawyer claimed the kid didn't realize the seriousness of his crime. Got him off with ninety days and two years' probation."

"So what happened?"

"He missed his probation appointment and Gus got worried. He's got a sixth sense when something's going south and he wanted me to see what I could find out about Wade. Like you, Gus thinks he's basically a good kid and something just isn't right."

"Sounds like Gus' instincts are on target. I haven't heard anything, but I know the family's address. They've got a little farm about five miles from Azle. If Wade's hiding, there's plenty of places to get lost out there. I'll get you the address."

"Thanks, Fred." Kelly stood and followed him over to the register.

"Here's the address. And, I want to know what you find out. Don't be such a stranger. You don't have to wait until you're trying to track a bad guy before you stop in and chew the fat."

"You got it, bud. Thanks. And damn, that car's hot." Kelly took the note with the address, and made a mental note to spend an afternoon with Fred next chance he got.

Now it's time to get my butt on back to ranch and check in with my bride. Kelly figured he'd get an early start for Azle in the morning. Tonight, he had a honeymoon to plan, something that he admitted was more than a little overdue. *I need to talk to Gillian about picking up something special for Stella while we're on this trip. That gal can be a right pain in the ass when she wants to, but I have to give her credit, she sure came up with a good one this time.*

Jake, the German Shepherd who'd adopted Kelly back when he lived alone in his cabin at Indian Creek, met the truck with a chorus of yips and yaps. Kelly got out of the cab and stopped to scratch behind Jake's ears, all the while admiring the view on the porch. Gillian had a couple of plates in one hand and a pitcher of tea in the other.

He reached the porch in a couple of strides and relieved her of the pitcher.

"Hey, you." Her blue eyes twinkled at him.

"Hey yourself." He let his gaze travel the length of her figure. Blonde hair flowed over her shoulders. She wore it pulled back most days, but knew how much he loved it loose, and usually tried to accommodate him in the evenings. "I was just thinking what a damn lucky guy I am."

She laughed. "Can you smell the enchiladas from there? I put extra cheese on top, just the way you like 'em."

With one last pat to Jake's head, he ascended the stairs to the porch. "Sweet tea, too."

"Again, just the way you like it."

Kelly took the plates from her hands and set them on the swing. He put the pitcher beside the glasses stacked on the small table next to the swing, then he drew her into his arms. "Everything about you is just the way I like it." Leaning in, he brushed back her hair and nibbled the nape of her neck. At the same time, he fumbled with the knot she'd tied in her shirt at the waist. "Except you have on way too many clothes."

He slid his hands under the crisp cotton blouse and over the white camisole she wore underneath.

Gillian melted against him. "You know we can fix that. I just thought you'd like to eat first. We need to talk about our trip, too."

He straightened her cami and retied the over-shirt. "You went to a lot of trouble to fix this delicious-looking dinner, I'd hate to get the blame for ruining it."

Smirking, she picked up their plates so they could sit, then handed him his. "But you'll take the blame for leaving me sexually frustrated?"

Kelly swallowed his first mouthful and smiled at his bride. He waved a finger at her. "Only for now. Remind me to check with you later and see if you still feel the same way."

She laughed. "I'm not worried."

He took another bite of food. "*I'm* worried, if you keep feeding me like this, I may have to go up a size."

Her eyes twinkled again. "I finished my shopping list for the trip, so it seemed like a tasty bribe would be in order."

Kelly scooped a healthy portion of salad onto his plate and passed the bowl to Gillian. "If you're gonna bribe me this good every time we take a trip, we might have to make it a regular thing."

"That other part, too." She nodded.

He grinned. "Seriously. Am I gonna to need to go shopping for this?"

"I don't think so. You've only worn your tux twice, and it looks fabulous. Those things never go out of style. The ACM is country and even your dress clothes are cowboy sporty. You've got more boots than a Texas bootmaker and you don't wear hats, so I'd say unless you want another shirt or a new sports coat, you're in good shape."

"Great. Then I'll leave you and Stella to take care of the shopping."

"And what are you going to be up to while we're buying out the malls?"

"I'm going to take an exciting little trip down to Azle in the morning."

"Azle? Who in the world goes to Azle?"

"I'm hoping my bail jumper. I talked to Fred yesterday and he recognized the guy's name. Seems Fred used to be best buds with Wade's older brother. The brother got sent to Afghanistan and never came back. The kid took it hard and got arrested for hacking into the Defense Department's computers. I'm kinda worried."

"I don't blame you. Does Wade have any reason to be mad at the government?"

"Fred remembers hearing something about Neil being deployed when he wasn't supposed to and he thinks maybe Wade blames the Army for killing his brother."

"That sounds bad. I'm glad you're going out there, Kelly. Hopefully you can do something before that boy gets himself into some serious trouble."

"Exactly. So let's finish eating and relax for a couple hours. I want to turn in early tonight."

"Fine by me. The vet is coming first thing in the morning so I've got an early call. Then I promised to go out to Stella's and try on her Valentino."

"Valentino, is it? Maybe I better bring along my six shooters. I've heard a thing or two about them Hollywood types."

"Oh, you!" Gillian giggled and batted her lashes in his direction. "Let's finish up here and I'll show you what type turns us Texas cowgirls on."

* * *

Gillian stepped inside of Stella's living room and gasped. "My God, you've really had it done." The back wall consisted of a solid sheet of glass that backed onto the greenhouse and gave the illusion that you'd stepped into a tropical garden. A sandstone fireplace glinted with specks of gold. Sunbeams played with crystal prisms dangling from a chandelier and reflecting back from the glass topped table.

"Like it?"

"*Like it?* It's amazing. Just as amazing as it was when I saw it up in y'all's honeymoon suite in Oregon. However did you manage to get it recreated here?"

Stella laughed. "At least there's some good came out of the Davis money. Cam won't let me use any of it for our living, but I was able to convince him decorating our home with no expense spared gave me so much pleasure it sort of made up for all the misery I suffered with that family."

Before their deaths Stella's husband, Andrew Davis and his niece Krystal Davis, heirs to the family fortune and major shareholders in the Davis Oil empire, had introduced Kelly and Stella. Future events and the tragedy surrounding both Andrew and Krystal started a chain of events that ended with Stella married to Kelly's best friend Cam Belcher, and the two families forever linked by the heartbreak and happiness of that fateful period in their lives.

Gillian slipped her arm around Stella's shoulder and hugged her friend. "You're right, and I'm glad Cam was smart enough to realize that. It's gorgeous."

Stella sniffed. "Thanks. I can always count on you. Now, what would you like to do first, eat, or try on the Valentino?"

"Let's eat." Gillian followed Stella into the kitchen. "I'd hate to try on the Valentino, find it was just an inch or so too small, and then feel too guilty to eat the fabulous luncheon I already know is waiting for me."

"Smart lady." Stella continued into the kitchen. "I haven't done much in here yet, just added the stainless steel appliances and that cooking island."

"And again, fabulous. I swear every time I come out here it's like you've done another major remodel. I love that cooking island, and the eating area down at the end is perfect, so inviting. It's great to sit here like this," Gillian hopped up onto one of the stools, "and watch your hostess prepare your meal."

Stella laid a place setting in front of Gillian and another one for herself. "It is, isn't it? This room's one of our favorites. The dining room is beautiful, of course, and we have a very nice breakfast nook." She pointed to the end of the room, where the kitchen jutted out towards the greenhouse and a charming wicker table set for two sported a colorful basket of fresh flowers. "Once I'm done here, we'll take our plates over there, but I know what you mean about this spot. Ninety percent of the time Cam and I end up perching on these stools, while we either both cook, or one of us cooks and the other samples."

With crab Caesars served and quickly consumed, and the last drop of Bloody Mary trickled down their throats, the women adjourned to Stella's dressing room.

"My one major indulgence since the Davis days," Stella explained, opening the door to a cedar lined room with floor to ceiling mirrors covering two walls. "I got used to having my own space for my clothes and being able to spend as much time as I needed picking out what I wanted. So when Cam and I started on the remodel of this house, I gave him carte blanche to do what he wanted with the entertainment room downstairs as long as he didn't object to this one."

"As if he would. But I have to confess, I'm surprised at you leaving yourself wide open to have your entertainment area, as you call it, plastered with portraits of every old time singer and actor that's ever graced a Western."

"Don't I know it, and you're right. That's exactly what's down there. Fortunately most of our friends are like you and Kelly, they're used to Cam and probably wouldn't believe they were in his house if there wasn't an excess of trivia everywhere they looked."

"You've got a point. Well however you managed it, I totally envy you this room. It's every woman's dream. Look at those shoes." Gillian gawked when Stella pulled open one of the mirrored doors to reveal a space about ten feet long and five feet wide, with every kind of shoe imaginable lining the walls. Dresses hung on long metal racks that rotated forward and spun around like the racks in a dry cleaning store. "There's no possible way one woman could wear all those shoes."

"Left over from my former days of grandeur." Stella grinned and reached for one of the garment bags that had swiveled into position.

"Here we go. See what you think."

Gillian's mouth fell open as she watched Stella lift the most gorgeous gown she'd ever seen out of the bag. She gasped in admiration as Stella spread out a gown so lovely it challenged the plumes of even the most elegant peacock.

"Oh my God. I've never seen anything so beautiful in my life. Stella, you can't really mean to loan me this gown when you've never even worn it yourself."

"Of course I'm not going to loan it to you. It's a gift. I want you to have it. Gillian, please don't argue with me. Meeting Kelly and you and finding Cam has changed my life. I have everything I've ever wanted and more. It gives me such pleasure to know that you're happy with this gown and that you'll accept it from me and wear it to those awards. Please don't turn me down."

"Oh, Stella." Gillian grabbed her friend and hugged her as tight as she could. "Of course I'll accept. I am just thrilled. It is beautiful."

"Well then, let's get it on you and see if it fits."

Minutes later Gillian spun around in front of the mirrors and Stella glowed with pride at the vision reflecting back at both of them. "Just what I thought. It's such a perfect fit, everyone will know it was made just for you. I wish I didn't have such big feet, you could have the shoes as well."

"Not to worry. I have a pair of strappy gold heels I've been saving for a long time now. They'll be perfect. Thank you again. You're quite a friend."

"I'm as happy as you are. Promise me you'll get a picture of you and Kelly at the awards and make a print for us."

"Done."

They retired to the comfy sitting room where they chatted until time for Gillian to get back to the ranch and check that evening chores had been done. "I really love having the after school kids working with me in the stables, but they're teenagers, it doesn't do to leave them too much on their own."

Stella laughed. "Point very well taken. Don't forget, pictures of you and Kelly with every celebrity you manage to drag in front of a camera."

"You got it."

As soon as she drove into the yard, Gillian went straight to the stables, pulled on the coveralls she kept handy in the shed beside the corral and headed for the barn. Jake, who'd been lying out in the afternoon sun, followed her.

"Kelly left you at home today did he, Jake? Must not have been sure what he was going to run into out there in Azle." Jake wagged his tail and headed up the path in front of Gillian.

At the barn she met up with Ben and Les, the two after school students who were her current part-timers. It helped a lot to have the teenagers muck out the barns and fill the mangers. That left her time to see to each of the horses individually, give out a few treats and spend some personal time with each of them.

Jake gave a couple of sharp barks from the end of the barn and Gillian moved down to join him. She told the student, "Saffron is still favoring that front leg of hers." She slid into the stall and ran her hand down the sore leg. "Dr. Susanna said just to keep an eye on it, and she'll be back in a couple of days to look again." Susanna was the new vet who replaced Dr. Morgan, the man whose name was permanently stricken from Gillian's vocabulary.

After another hour, Gillian finished up and she and Jake headed back to the house.

"Looks like I'm going to be eating alone." Gillian sat down in one of the rockers, but Jake lifted his head and sniffed the air, then let out a couple of short barks. "Or maybe not." She recognized his 'Kelly's coming' alert, and smiled in anticipation.

* * *

Jake met Kelly at the gate for his rubdown. "I've got a situation and I need to call Gus right away." Kelly leaned down and gave Gillian an 'I missed you' kiss. "I'll tell you all about it once I'm done, but it can't wait. I'll use your office phone, if that's okay."

"Of course. Go right ahead." Jake flopped at Gillian's feet and she reached down to scratch his ears. "We'll be right here waiting when you get done. Want me to get you a cold one?"

"Please. I'll be as quick as I can."

Gillian went to the kitchen for an ice bucket, covered a couple of long necks with crushed ice, heaped a plate with nacho chips, and homemade salsa. She grabbed a some dog treats out of Jake's drawer, loaded a tray and carried it out to the table in front of the swing.

"Here you go boy." She handed Jake one of his favorite chews, and settled down on the swing to wait for Kelly.

It took another fifteen minutes, but when he returned to the porch, his eyes lit up at the sight of the tray.

"Nice." He settled down beside Gillian, gave her an appreciative kiss on the lips and reached for one of the long necks.

"You're not going to believe what I ran into out there in Azle."

"I'm dying to know. It took all my will power not to sneak over to the office and listen outside the door."

Kelly laughed and ruffled her hair. "So, I have a little spy in the house."

Gillian gave him the look, the one that all men recognize as 'you better talk, now'.

"Okay," Kelly held up his hand. "Turn down the laser. Let me get a couple bites of these nachos and I'll tell you all about it."

She raised her eyebrows and kept her eyes on him while he chewed and swallowed and washed it down with a healthy swig of beer.

"I had a funny feeling about this Clements kid. I'm not sure what it was, but thinking back, there was something off in Fred's voice when he talked about the family. Nothing specific mind you, but just something that set my nerves tingling.

Kelly took another sip of his beer and set it on the table. "Anyway, I drove up to the house. Nothing more than an old shack really, but there was a car and an old pickup in the driveway, so I figured someone had to be around. I got out, knocked on the door, and waited. No answer, so I knocked again, harder. When there was still no answer I walked around to the back of the shack, but there didn't seem to be any sign of life.

"So of course you decided maybe you'd better get back into your truck and get out of there in case the inhospitables who weren't answering the door turned out to be really unfriendly." Gillian grinned.

"Well. I did check to make sure I had my thirty-eight in the glove box." He grinned back at her. "Anyway, there was an old dirt road that seemed to lead back into the property and I decided to follow it and see where it took me. Damn good thing I just had Old Blue tuned up. We rolled down that road so quiet you'd have had to be listening for us in order to know we were coming."

"I take it you found something that made you glad you hadn't made any noise."

"I was about ready to turn around when I heard what sounded like a military platoon on a training mission."

"Oh no."

"Oh yes. I turned off the truck, got out and followed the sound on foot. I'll be damned if I wasn't right. It was a military training mission, but it sure as hell wasn't our military."

"Not terrorists?"

"Damn sure looked like it to me. I snapped off a couple of pictures with my cell phone and then got the hell out of there. I don't think they heard anything. Hells bells, they were making so much noise the Texas Guard could have snuck up on them, but I didn't waste any time making tracks out of there."

"So you think Wade Clements has gotten himself mixed up with a terrorist cell?"

"It looks that way. Anyhow, that's way above my pay grade. I told Gus everything I knew, and sent him the pictures. That's as far as it's going to go with me. I reminded him we were set to leave town this week and from the looks of things out there in Azle, Gus'll turn the whole mess over to the Texas National Guard, and they'll take over from there."

"I'm glad we're leaving town." Gillian snuggled into Kelly's arms. "I know it's selfish of me, but even the thought of you dealing with terrorists scares me to death. Those people aren't normal. They pretend they're acting for a God, but even their own faith rejects them. They're not acting for anyone but themselves."

"I don't want you to worry about anything." Kelly pulled Gillian into his arms and kissed her until she relaxed against his chest. "We're going to Hollywood and we're going to have ourselves a honeymoon that'll rival the Kardashians, and then we're going to Vegas and paint the town."

"Oh please." Gillian burst out laughing. "You really don't want us to end up the laughing stock of Fort Worth."

He waggled his eyebrows. "You know what they say, *'What Happens in Vegas Stays in Vegas'*."

Gillian grinned and snuggled her face against his neck.

Chapter Two

In the travel magazine Kelly read on the plane, the writer described Beverly Hills as a 'mix of cosmopolitan sophistication and star-studded excitement'. From what he could see as they whisked along Wilshire Boulevard and turned onto Rodeo Drive, Kelly figured it lived up to its name. Gillian's nose stayed glued to the window from the time they left the airport until they pulled into what the driver called the *Porte cochère*--the passage between the two wings of the hotel.

When Kelly and Gillian got out of the limo they were met by a doorman in top hat and tails. "Definitely posh," Kelly whispered in Gillian's ear.

The lobby beat description. Flowers, sculpted glass, and a chandelier with more lights than the Hideaway lit up for a Saturday night shindig. Kelly had to admit the word elegance fit this place like a glove.

"Can you believe this?" Gillian, eyes round as giant marbles, squeezed his arm.

"Kinda takes your breath away." They stood under the chandelier, caught in the magic of lights reflecting on the marble beneath their feet.

"Mr. McWinter." A bellman magically appeared at their side and stood discreetly waiting for them to close their mouths. "Everything is prepared for your arrival." He smiled at both of them and spoke to Kelly. "If you and Mrs. McWinter would like to follow me, I'll see you to your suite."

They followed him across the lobby, gawking all the way. The elevator whisked them to the twelfth floor where they stepped out into a hallway lined with portraits of movie star greats from days gone by.

"Mrs. Fischer mentioned that you'd want to be connected to the pool and spa," the bellman stopped in front of one of the doors at the end of the hall. "I hope you'll like this corner Beverly Suite. As you can see, it has two balconies with a nice view from either."

Their escort checked the rooms, made sure all their luggage was accounted for, and reminded them to call if they needed anything.

"Nice. Did he say nice?" Gillian whispered when the door closed behind him. "I guess in his world looking directly out on shoppers strolling along world famous Rodeo Drive is just nice."

"You can talk out loud you know. I expect this room is insulated for sound." Kelly laughed and Gillian poked him in the ribs.

"Okay, wise guy. And just how many times have you looked out your window at women flicking their chinchillas over their shoulders?"

"Yep, they do beat anything I've ever seen. It must be eighty degrees out there, and everywhere I look there's a cougar with a rat around her neck stalking a billionaire."

"Kelly McWinter, you stop mocking. Did you see the bar we passed? The place was probably packed with movie stars and millionaires."

Kelly grabbed Gillian around the waist, backed up to the bed and rolled with her onto the ultra-soft mattress of their King sized bed. "I'm a lot more interested in what I've got right here in my own room than what they've got down there in the bar. Not arguing, just saying it's a lot more likely there's cougars and tourists looking for stars and rich folks."

Gillian gave up and flopped back in his arms. "Did I hear the majordomo say we had champagne and strawberries in the sitting room?"

"You stay right here." Kelly gave her a quick kiss and headed out to get the goodies. When he returned, Gillian had stripped out of her traveling clothes and was lying on her side beneath a satin sheet. "Mmm, and I thought the strawberries looked good."

He set the silver tray on the nightstand, along with the bottle of bubbly and two glasses. "Although, I could do without champagne. Beer suits me just fine." Shrugging out of his jacket, he hung it on the back of a nearby chair and proceeded to kick out of the rest of his clothes.

Gillian poured them each a glass but they both kept their eyes on one another.

When he dropped his boxers and his erection sprang forward, she smiled wickedly. "That's not for the champagne, then."

"Not even close." Kelly stroked his shaft and moved to the side of the bed.

She took a sip then set her glass aside. Popping a strawberry between her teeth, she nodded backwards for him to come and get it.

Kelly tossed the sheet back and his cock twitched when he saw her gorgeous naked body sprawled across the bed. He straddled her and leaned down, biting off half of the berry in her mouth. He chewed for a moment then pressed their lips together for a sticky, sweet kiss.

She groaned and thrust her hips upward.

He liked her way of thinking. They had all night, but he needed to take the edge off. Kissing her earlobe he whispered, "I plan to eat more of those strawberries, and a few other things, here shortly. But right now I need you." He pressed his erection against her belly. "Need to be inside you."

"I need that too, sugar." She reached between them and guided him home. "Take me, hard and fast. Then after you're done eating my...berries...I'm going to drizzle bubbly in your belly button and all parts south, and lick it off."

A shiver raced down Kelly's spine and he thrust deeply. "Damn, you keep talking like that and I won't last long."

She cupped his neck and pulled his face down to meet hers. "I don't need long, darlin'. I just need one good thrill. I know for a fact you can manage that." She kissed him, pressing her tongue into his mouth.

Kelly groaned this time, and soon had to pull away to gasp for air. "You'll get more than one if I have my way."

Gillian grinned at him lazily. "Aw, sugar, don't you always get your way?"

He grinned through gritted teeth. "Funny, I thought *you* always got your way."

She caressed the back of his neck, her body moving in rhythm with his. "Isn't it good that we both want the same things, then?"

He caught the mischievous glint in her eye, and it nearly sent him over the edge. He had no intention of going without her, though. "So good," he agreed, ramping up his thrusts. "So, so good."

She kissed him again then murmured, "Come on, lover. I'm close. Very close."

Kelly drove forward a few more times until he saw her eyes roll back in her head. Her low, keening moan told him exactly what he needed to know. He could relax and let it happen. "Fuck, yeah," he murmured, and shattered.

Gillian held on for the ride, then eventually grabbed his face and kissed him hard. "I love it when you talk dirty to me during sex."

He grinned, attempting to catch his breath. "I love whatever you love. I just plain love you."

She sighed contentedly, and smoothed a hand over his jawline. "I just plain love you, too."

* * *

Several hours later after all their desires were fulfilled, followed by a long and leisurely nap, Kelly woke up with Gillian snuggled in his arms.

"Wow," he whispered into her ear. "If anyone had told me a woman could do that with strawberries and champagne I'd have called them a liar."

Gillian opened her eyes and gazed at him lazily. "Never mind that, what I want to know is where in the devil did you get that feather?"

"You liked that did you? One of these days I'll have to introduce you to Deputy Randy Buffalo. He's a Comanche Indian, traces his line all the way back to Chief Buffalo Hump. We worked a case together while I was still on the force. He was tracking a suspect from Amarillo and I was tracking one from Fort Worth and damned if they didn't come together in El Paso. We took them down on a Friday night and had to hang around waiting for a judge until Monday morning. I don't remember a lot about that weekend, but I do recall a bet on who could swallow the first worm. I won the bet and Randy gave me the magic feather. He told me not to use the feather until I found a woman I wanted forever. I put it away in my stuff and never thought about it again. Then the other night when I was looking for a set of turquoise cufflinks I bought in El Paso, I came across the feather. It seemed like this might be a good time to try out Randy's magic, so I brought it along."

Gillian wrapped one of her legs around Kelly's waist and grinned. "I bet that Comanche friend of yours is a married man with half a dozen kids by now. At least he is if he kept one of those feathers for himself."

Kelly chuckled. "You're probably right. And as much as I hate to say this, we probably need to get cleaned up and out of here. Marcy should be getting in soon, and we'll need to meet her."

"Oh, I know it. Give me one more kiss then I'll go take a quick shower."

He did as directed, fingering her nipple as they kissed. When he pulled away he asked, "Do you actually know the meaning of a 'quick' shower?"

She swatted his chest then climbed out of bed. "Watch it, buster."

"I'd rather watch you and that fine ass. Hate to see you go, but love to watch you leave."

Grinning, she squeezed her breasts with both hands then scampered into the bath.

Happy as hell, Kelly stretched out on the bed while Gillian showered. Halfway into an impromptu nap, his cell phone rang with Marcy's version of *Texas When I Die*.

"You made it," he said when Marcy's smiling face lit up his iPhone screen.

"I did, no problems. How are y'all? Did you get settled in your room? Do you like it?"

"We are, and we do. You hit a home run with this place."

"Good. I figured you'd like it best being close to the pool and spa and all. We're upstairs in the skyloft. Hollywood stuff, you know. My manager insisted. It's a secured floor and I need to give you an access code and we can maybe talk about the weekend."

"Sure. Just say when."

"I was hoping you and Gillian could join us for drinks in an hour. My sister Rachel is with me, do you remember her?"

"I do. It's great she could make it."

"She was so excited. I can't wait to introduce her to Gillian."

"Sounds like a plan. I'd like a bit of time to discuss your schedule and figure out where you want us to be and when, stuff like that." They firmed up the details and ended the call.

"That was Marcy." Kelly tossed his phone on the nightstand and joined Gillian at the dressing table. "Her sister, Rachel, came with her and she can't wait to introduce you."

"I didn't know she had a sister. How old is she?"

He scratched his head. "I'd say about twenty-one. Pretty sure Cam said she was going to college in Arlington. Something like that. You can ask her."

"I will. Right now I'm going to finish my makeup and get dressed. What time does she want to meet?"

"In an hour. I'll take my shower now, before the sight of you gives me more ideas." He grinned and leaned down to plant a kiss on her bare shoulder. "Too late. Want to get back in and join me?"

Gillian turned her head and placed a kiss on his lips. "I'll take a rain check. Now hop in the shower so I can concentrate on getting dressed."

He reluctantly obliged, and an hour later, dressed in casual evening wear, Kelly escorted Gillian through the lobby to the presidential elevator. Giving his credentials to the attendant and waiting while the man called upstairs, they were soon whisked to the eighth floor of the Wilshire wing and escorted along a hallway lined with roman columns and extravagant floral arrangements. Graceful ferns swept the gleaming wood floors. The attendant knocked lightly and the door swung open.

Marcy stood in the doorway. "Kelly! Gillian!. I'm so glad you're finally here. Oh my God! I haven't seen you two since Aunt Stella's wedding." Dressed in red silk lounging pajamas, her shining black hair tied back with a matching red scarf, Marcy's eyes sparkled with delight as she hugged them both and urged them into the suite.

"Wow," Gillian gasped, turning full circle to take in the sky-lit grand entrance leading into a majestic living room with wraparound windows on three sides, a cozy library and a formal dining room with an adjoining kitchenette.

"I know. Definitely Hollywood." Marcy's musical laughter brought smiles to both of them. "Come on. I want you to meet Rachel." She waved her hand towards a plush suede loveseat flanking the window with a view of Rodeo Drive. "Of course the studio insisted I have a maid. I'll have her bring you a drink while I get Rachel. She was taking a nap, but I promised to wake her as soon as you got here. Would you like champagne?"

Kelly looked at Gillian, who quickly nodded her head. "Yes please. If I left it to Kelly he'd be ordering a long neck, but we'd love some champagne. Wouldn't we?"

Kelly nodded and laughed. "Of course. I've been dying for some of that fancy bubbly ever since we got here."

Both women laughed at what was obviously a bald-faced lie, and Marcy picked up the phone on the counter and placed their order. "I'll be right back."

Before long, a smiling young Mexican woman entered the suite wheeling a serving cart that contained a bottle of champagne chilling in a silver bucket, glasses and a selection of hors d'oeuvres on silver trays.

"Nice." Kelly stood to check out the platters. "Want some of these?" He added a couple of shrimp, puffed pastry squares, two pieces of sushi from a California roll and a scoop of guacamole to one of the serving plates.

"You'll spoil your dinner," Gillian chided.

"You know better than that." He placed a napkin over Gillian's knees and set the plate on the table in front of them. "If you don't help I'll have half this spread cleaned up and still have lots of room for that Keller's buttermilk fried chicken at Bouchon. Marcy pulled some strings to get us a reservation there tonight and I'm definitely bringing my appetite. He only serves it the first and third Monday of the month, and this is the third. I can taste it already."

Gillian chuckled and they both glanced up when Marcy returned.

"Sorry it took us so long." Marcy entered the room followed by a younger and lighter version of herself. Rachel, who looked the same except maybe a little taller since the last time Kelly had seen her, smiled a hello to Kelly. Rachel, a slim young lady as blonde as her sister was dark, smiled with the same snapping brown eyes as her sister.

"Rachel, you remember Aunt Stella's friend Kelly McWinter, don't you? And this is his wife, Gillian."

Rachel held out her hand to Gillian and smiled. "It's nice to meet you." Her voice, softer than Marcy's, resonated with the same lyrical quality. She turned to Kelly and titled her head back to look into his eyes. "It's good to see you again. I never had a chance to thank you for looking after my sister the way you did. I don't know what I'd do without Marcy. Thank you so much."

Kelly nodded. "You're very welcome. It was definitely my pleasure. Your sister's the most delightful client I've ever had. Next to this one over here." He nodded at Gillian and flashed a big smile. "I'm a lucky guy."

"So, I imagine you're both anxious for a rundown on our itinerary." Marcy and Rachel sat together on the couch facing the couple. "You know of course that we're in the middle of the most fantastic shopping area on the west coast?"

Kelly groaned and Gillian chuckled.

"Oh don't worry, Kelly. That wasn't aimed at you. I've got a dozen meetings all over town tomorrow, so it looks like you're stuck tagging along with me. Mark's made me promise not to go anywhere at all without you, and considering that nut job scared the life out of me when he almost made it to my bedroom, I'm not one for arguing. Probably means some boring times for you, but it was Gillian and Rachel I was thinking about."

She flashed a big smile at Gillian and reach for Rachel's hand. "I thought the two of you might enjoy a chauffeur-driven limo to whisk you along Rodeo Drive and hit all the Beverly Hills hot spots the celebrities are so fond of – you never know who you'll meet on one of those outings. The studio is sending a car for Kelly and I, and the hotel has put a car and chauffeur at my disposal. What do you say? Would you enjoy that?" Marcy aimed a questioning glance at Gillian.

"Would we?" Gillian grinned. "I don't know about you Rachel, but that sounds absolutely decadent to my ears."

"Oh me, too. Would you really go shopping and sightseeing with me?"

"Are you kidding? I'd be thrilled. Frankly, Kelly is the world's worst sight seer, and I've been wondering how I'd manage to slip away from him and do some exploring." The two women smiled at each other like a couple of guilty kids sharing a secret.

"I think we're all set." Gillian nodded to Marcy. "We love your idea."

Marcy beamed. "That's great, then. Kelly, you and I will need to leave by eight-thirty, my first meeting is in Studio City at nine-thirty, and you know LA traffic."

"Gotcha. Sounds like things will work out great. Gilly and I will spend the rest of the day settling in, and tonight we're out to dinner at Bouchon. If you'll buzz me when you're ready in the morning I'll meet you downstairs."

"Excellent. Gillian, perhaps you'd like to join Rachel up here for breakfast and the two of you can plan out your day?"

"Perfect. What do you think Rachel, is nine o'clock a good time?"

"Definitely. I'll have breakfast ordered up and we can take our time and make plans, then we can order the limo. This is going to be super fun." The young girl's eyes sparkled, and Gillian's enthusiasm matched her excitement.

"Great." Kelly rose and extended a hand to Gillian. "We'll see you in the morning." He smiled at Marcy and nodded his head to Rachel.

Leading his wife out, he waited until the sisters were out of earshot before he spoke again. "That was awfully nice of you to step up to the plate with Rachel the way you did." Kelly rubbed the palm of Gillian's hand as they waited for the elevator.

"Not at all. I'm quite excited about the prospect of a chauffeur driven limousine shopping tour of Beverly Hills. Of course, there's a very strong possibility I'll be putting a major dent in the family budget."

Kelly laughed. "Oh, I think the old stash under the mattress can handle a few hefty withdrawals. You go ahead and have the time of your life. That's the one thing I want from this trip more than anything else."

Gillian stood on tiptoe and kissed his lips. "You've already made sure of that, you know. You're special."

"You're pretty special yourself. And just so you know, I'll take you shopping anytime you want me to."

"Thanks, but I know you'd be miserable if I dragged you along shopping and sightseeing and I do want to see LA and all the tourist attractions. It'll be great having Rachel with me, and you'll be able to concentrate on Marcy without having to worry about either one of us. It's what's called a win/win situation."

"Then we're agreed. I still think you deserve an extra special treat. It's our honeymoon after all, and I intend to spoil you rotten."

Gillian cocked her head and gave him *the look*. "Okay, buster. What are you talking about?"

"Me? What could I possibly be talking about?" Kelly knew he appeared about as innocent as a five year old with his hand stuck in the cookie jar.

His text notification sounded and he glanced at the screen.

Tomorrow night at eight works for me. Wolfgang Puck's LA Live work for you?

He texted back quickly. *Sounds great. Looking forward to it. Thanks.*

Kelly glanced up and saw Gillian eyeing him suspiciously.

"Okay, big boy. Fess up. Who was that text from?"

"That text? Oh, that was Blake Shelton. He's in town filming The Voice and he's going to meet us, Marcy and Rachel, for dinner tomorrow night. You okay with that?"

"Oh, my freaking hell! You've got to be kidding me! You actually made a date with Blake Shelton?" Gillian, who Kelly knew to be one of the most fanatical Blake Shelton fans in the known universe, leaped into Kelly's arms and wrapped her legs around his waist.

Chuckling, he cupped her ass while she gave him a kiss that curled his toes.

Chapter Three

"I can't believe we're cruising down Rodeo Drive in this awesome limo." Rachel practically bounced in her seat, turning right and left, taking in every store they passed. "Look at those storefronts! Tiffany, Prada, Gucci, Valentino, Armani, Versace, Lanvin, Jimmy Choo."

Gillian laughed and leaned up close to the excited girl. "I know. They're fabulous. I can hardly wait to go inside. So, where do you want to start?"

Rachel's eyes sparkled. "Marcy gave me a gift certificate to Jimmy Choo's. I'm so excited I can't breathe. Can we start there?"

"You bet. I'm pretty jazzed myself, although I probably won't be able to find any cowboy boots."

Rachel's eyes flew open, and Gillian grabbed her in a hug. "Just kidding. I've always wanted to browse one of those designer shoe stores. Let's go find the perfect pair of Jimmy Choo's for you."

Two hours later, after trying on what Gillian figured amounted to twenty-five pairs of shoes, she and Rachel finally exited Jimmy Choo's with Rachel holding tight to her precious bag.

"I absolutely cannot believe I own these Fayme's. Oh my God, they were almost a thousand dollars! I'm never going to be able to thank Marcy enough. I'm saving them, you know. For my graduation from Nashville State next spring. I wanted to start at UT Arlington my first two years, but Dad and Marcy about had a fit, so we compromised on two years at Nashville State and then off to UT Arlington. Where you can be absolutely certain Aunt Stella will find a way to keep me on a very close rein."

"Are you interested in following your sister into the entertainment field?"

"Not on your life. I couldn't stand all those people hounding me everywhere I went. The paparazzi can be completely horrible. Actually, I love horses and the whole equine industry. I've been taking courses in animal husbandry. There is no specific degree, so I'm going to go ahead and get my BS. At the same time I'll try to get into a certified training program and maybe get on as a working student with one of the commercial stables."

Gillian grinned. "Did your sister happen to tell you what I do? Or for that matter, I wonder if she even knows?"

"I don't think she's ever mentioned it. Do you like horses?"

Gillian threw back her head and practically snorted with laughter. "Now you talk about the universe taking charge of things sometimes, it just so happens that I'm the owner of Lake Country Stables in Fort Worth. I'm also on the board of the Tarrant County Equine Society, and we often recruit promising new trainers. I'd say you and I are going to have a lot to talk about."

Rachel's eyes bugged until they looked like they might pop out of the sockets. "I don't believe this! Life is so funny. I swear Gillian, I never even thought to ask what you did. I knew Kelly was a PI and I guess I just figured you managed his office."

"Oh, I believe you. I have a very high respect for arrangements made by greater powers. Now let's get back to our shopping trip. What else are we going to do?"

"I hope you won't think I'm horribly spoiled, but Marcy also gave me a gift certificate for Versace. I'm going to see if I can find my graduation dress there. Do you think that'll be over the top?"

"Your sister loves you and she wants you to have something really, really special for your graduation. Of course you're not spoiled. Look at how much you appreciate her gifts. Now, before we head over to Versace – where I suspect we're going to try on an awful lot of dresses finding exactly the right match for those satin and ivory sandals you have there. How about *Poisson* for lunch? Marcy called while you were paying for your shoes and she said she'd book a reservation for us. I browsed their menu, listen to this." She scrolled through her phone. "Here are some of the highlights: *tomato bisque, spicy tuna tartar, cheese platter, Kobe burger, seafood salad, penne arrabbiata, roasted salmon* – anything strike your fancy?"

"Wow. Everything. Gillian, that sounds perfect. But what about you? So far this has been all about me. What do you want to do?"

"Eat." Gillian laughed. "And I'm rather intrigued with your Versace visit. I've a mind to pick up a little surprise for Kelly while I'm there, so don't you worry about me. It's like having a little sister – which unfortunately I never had – watching you shop for your graduation outfit. I'm thrilled that I'm getting to share this with you. We'd better hurry though, our reservation is for noon and it's almost that already. Let's go see if we can pick out anybody famous."

They headed to the limo for the ride to *Poisson.*

Once the driver had deposited them, they climbed the steps to the restaurant.

"I wonder if that paparazzi was following us," Rachel whispered.

"Where?"

"Don't turn around. See all those guys standing by the curb?"

"I see them. Are they paparazzi?"

"I think so, they've got all that camera stuff on their shoulders. They must be waiting for somebody famous."

Gillian tried to appear nonchalant. "What makes you think one of them was following us?

"Not there. Just look casually over your shoulder. See, the man with the *Go Navy* T-shirt and the tight black jeans?"

"Yes. Why do you think he's following us?"

"He was outside the door when we left Jimmy Choo's. Then I saw him jump on a motor scooter and now he's here. It just seems like he was following us."

"But he doesn't have a camera."

Rachel shrugged. "Just strange, is all."

"I agree. Not saying you're wrong." Gillian laughed. "I'm usually the first one to be suspicious. I figured that came from living with a detective. I'm sure he's just another tourist, probably as excited about Rodeo Drive as we are. Come on, let's go inside."

"It looks crowded."

"Shouldn't be a problem with the reservation Marcy made."

"Ohhh, maybe that's why the guy's been following us. Maybe he thinks Marcy's going to join us."

"I wish she could, but she and Kelly are completely booked until this afternoon. Don't worry, dinner will make up for it."

The girl's eyes lit up. "Where are we having dinner?"

Gillian smiled. "Apparently it's a surprise. You'll find out later. Right now, let's focus on lunch."

Rachel let out a gasp and grabbed Gillian's hand pulling her up the steps to *Poisson*. "Did you see that? Ellen just went inside. Oh Gillian, I just love Ellen."

The meal was a star-studded event with several celebrity sightings. Gillian chuckled at Rachel's giddiness but had to admit she was having a grand time, too.

"My seafood salad was awesome." Rachel put her napkin on the table and smiled at Gillian. "Did you like your Kobe burger?"

"I loved it. I've been wanting to try it for a long time. You know how we are about our beef in Texas. It's practically sacrilege to order the Japanese stuff." Gillian shoved her plate away from the edge of the table. "You have to promise not to tell Kelly."

"Cross my heart. Oh look, Ellen's getting ready to leave. I bet those paparazzi will go crazy with their cameras."

"Here's our waiter. I'll take care of the bill and we'll follow her out. Maybe we can catch some of the excitement."

The black-clad man approached their table. "Mrs. McWinter. You enjoyed your lunch?"

"It was delicious. If we can have the bill now, we're going to sneak out behind Ellen and watch the camera frenzy."

"Ah, of course. We've enjoyed having you, but no need to worry about the charges. Mrs. Fischer has taken care of everything."

"Oh, that Marcy. She's too generous. At least let me leave your tip."

"Thank you, no. That has also been attended to. If you hurry, you should be just in time to watch Ellen's departure. She's heading for the door."

"Thank you." Gillian smiled up at the waiter and stood.

Rachel jumped from her seat. "Hurry, Gillian, there she goes now."

"Here, let me carry your bag." Gillian reached out for the shoe bag and smiled as Rachel raced for the door.

"Look. The paparazzi are going crazy." Rachel stood on the steps watching the swarm of photographers snapping their cameras. A few car lengths up the block another limo stood waiting while Ellen generously posed for the snapping flashbulbs and smiled for the cameras.

"I wonder what's going on there." Gillian motioned to where their driver seemed to be having an altercation with the young man in the *Go Navy* T-shirt. Gillian turned to Rachel. "You stay here and watch Ellen. I'll go check out what's going on with our driver. I'll be right back."

"Take your time. I'm having a ball." Rachel stepped down to the bottom of the stairs and leaned against the wrought iron railing to watch the paparazzi ply their trade.

After fifteen minutes of negotiating between the limo driver and the young man, Gillian managed to facilitate a truce. The driver insisted he had *not* bumped the scooter, and the irate man just as vehemently insisted the driver had gotten too close and put a dent in his back fender. Gillian managed to convince the fellow that nothing good would come of calling the police and creating a spectacle. Her offer of a hundred dollar bill was accepted. Both men agreed to let the matter end there, and she turned to call Rachel.

The girl wasn't on the steps.

"I'll just be a minute," she told the limo driver. "Rachel probably went back inside to use the restroom. I'll get her and we'll be on our way.

Returning to *Poisson*, she paused to query the hostess, but the woman couldn't recall seeing Rachel come back.

"She might have slipped by in the confusion." The girl lowered her voice to a whisper. "Usher and his party slipped in while the paparazzi were busy chasing Ellen. Naturally that caused a buzz amongst some of our out-of-town clientele." She smiled again. "I'm afraid those of us who see them everyday tend to get a bit blasé about our celebrities, but they're a real treat for our visitors. Don't get me wrong, we're very happy for their patronage. It's just a bit distracting at times, and I'm afraid this was one of them. Please do check the washrooms, and I'll ask the staff is anyone noticed the young lady return." She pointed Gillian in the direction of the ladies' room.

After a quick trip through the swanky spot which was as big as some people's living rooms, she was able to determine Rachel wasn't in there.

Damn, I didn't get her cell number. Why didn't I think of that? Gillian pulled her cell out of her bag and dialed Kelly's number. The call went straight to voicemail. *I could send him a text, but that's silly. I'm sure Rachel's close by. She probably just wandered further than she intended.*

"Kelly McWinter here," his voice spoke in her ear. "I can't take your call now, but y'all leave a number and I'll get back to you quick as I can."

Gillian smiled, no mistaking the Texas in his voice. "Hi hon, sorry to bug you, but there was a bit of excitement between our limo driver and an idiot on a scooter. I went over to help while Rachel waited in front of the restaurant. Trouble is now I can't find her. She seems to have wandered off while I was straightening out the mess with the limo driver. I didn't think to get her cell number this morning. Sorry, that was dumb. I hate to bother you but if you could text me the number that would be great. Love you." She returned the phone to her purse and headed back outside.

Now where in the heck could that girl have gone? Gillian pulled out the map of Rodeo Drive she'd picked up from the hotel lobby that morning and glanced at the shops listed along the Drive.

Michael Kors, of course. Rachel mentioned she wanted to look at some jeans. I bet she went in there just to look around for a minute while I was tied up.

Gillian stuck the map back in her bag and walked over to the limo. She opened the passenger door and stuck her head inside. "My young friend seems to have disappeared so I'm going to take a walk down the Drive and see if I can spot her."

"Okay, ma'am. I'll wait right here."

"Thanks, and if you don't mind, keep an eye out for her. If she comes back while I'm gone please ask her to wait in the car until I get back. I won't be long."

"Sure thing."

Gillian shut the door and took off down the sidewalk as fast as her long legs and Texas cowgirl boots would carry her.

What seemed like hours later Gillian had a knot in the pit of her stomach, and her head throbbed with a headache to end all headaches. She'd looked everywhere. Rachel wasn't in Michael Kors. The nearby hotel had proven to be a bad guess, they didn't even have a back entrance. Gillian had gone back to Jimmy Choo's then all the way over to Versace, just in case Rachel had gotten tired of waiting and ventured out on her own. *She's not that kind of girl.* Gillian knew it was stupid but she couldn't quit looking. She didn't want to face the inevitable. *I've lost Rachel in the middle of Beverly Hills.* How could she have been so stupid? Whatever possessed her to leave that young girl on the steps of the restaurant alone while she dealt with that scooter idiot?

Back at the limo the driver reported there'd been no sign of Rachel. Gillian grabbed her cell and tried not to cry as she typed the text.

SOS! NOW!

* * *

Kelly leaned against the hall wall of KDEN, Santa Monica's premiere country music station, opposite the big wall sign that implored visitors to "Let us take you down some country roads!" He resisted the urge to laugh at the sign. *Hell, yeah, Santa Monica really knew what a country road was like.* He pulled out his phone to take advantage of fifteen free minutes while Marcy did her interview. *Well, damn.* Missed call from Gus. One from Gillian too, but Gus wouldn't have called if something wasn't up. *Better take care of that first.*

Gus answered on the first ring.

"Your hat still fit your head now that you're hobnobbing with all them celebrities?"

"I don't wear hats, remember?"

"You get my point."

"Been here one day, I don't think my head's in danger of changing shape anytime soon. What you got for me?"

"Didn't you tell me the only actual building you saw out in Azle at the Clements place was an old shack?"

"Yeah, but I didn't really take the time to look around once I scoped out that squad of home-grown crazies firing AK-47's. For damn sure, all them weren't bunking in that shack. Why you askin'?"

"Cause three families have filed missing kids reports from that area in the last twenty-four hours. Now, coincidence is coincidence but—"

"Liar. You don't believe in coincidence."

Gus laughed. "Nope, damn sure don't. Not when all three kids are teen-aged males aged fifteen to sixteen who're reportedly real tight with each other."

"Which means they could've just decided to have a wild night out together that got out of hand and now they're scared to come home."

"Yeah, it could. But it don't feel right. 'Cause see, one of those boys lost a brother in Afghanistan. And the other two lost their dads in Iraq. And their moms all say these boys are living for the day they're old enough to enlist. That's the primary reason they're all such good friends in the first place. They don't seem to be wild kids, not even bad kids, but they're kind of—*fanatical*—I guess is the word I'm looking for. Focused. *Save the world and death to the enemy* type kids, you know what I'm sayin'?"

"The type of kids who'd be real easy for militia-survivalist groups to recruit."

"Give the man a cigar."

"Which actually sounds damn good, but don't tell Gillian, she'd shoot me. I didn't think about it at the time, but that first building I saw was more of an outpost. Sorta like a line shack. Can't imagine any family actually living in it, the main ranch house is almost certainly further back. Pull the property plats from the Tax Assessor's office. You need to know exactly how big a land spread you're dealing with."

"Got somebody on that already. There was only that one dirt road you followed on back till you heard the gunfire?"

"Yeah, but if they're actually big enough to be a recruitment-training facility, they've hidden any old roads back into the property that'd lead to the stronghold. Or I would, anyway."

"Always been grateful you're one of the good guys, that's for damn sure. Hate to tangle with you from the other side."

Kelly laughed. "Yeah, right backatcha', old man."

"Watch who you're callin' old, boy."

The insistent ding of an incoming text made Kelly lower the phone from his ear to view the screen. Gillian. The fine hairs on the back of his neck stood straight up and came to attention.

"I gotta go, Gus, check in with you later."

* * *

Gillian climbed into the back of the limo and put her head in her hands. The SOS would do it. She and Kelly had their own code. She would never send him an SOS unless it was truly an emergency. No matter what her husband was doing, he'd get back to her immediately.

She'd no sooner covered her face than the lyrics to *Sangria* started playing on her phone. Grabbing the phone again, she punched the talk button. "Kelly. Oh my God. She's gone. I can't find her anywhere."

"Rachel?"

"Yes, Rachel! Of course, Rachel! She's the only one I'm with."

His sigh was audible. "Gill, take a deep breath and tell me what happened."

She tried to reel herself in, but it was next to impossible. "I did tell you, in my voicemail. It's like I said. She just disappeared."

"Honey, I haven't listened to it yet. I called the minute I got your SOS. Please,

64

just go ahead and give me all the details. Don't leave anything out."

"Kelly, I need you here!"

"We're on our way, sugar. The driver is heading to Beverly Hills. Marcy and I will be with you soon. She just finished signing the contracts to appear on an episode of Nashville."

Gillian's head was spinning. "Oh, God. If only this hadn't happened I'd be so excited."

"It's okay. Now relax, clear your mind, and tell me everything both of you did from the time you left the hotel this morning."

Gillian took a deep breath. She steadied herself and recounted the day.

"We got here about eleven o'clock and went straight to Jimmy Choo's. Rachel was really excited about a gift certificate and she wanted to pick out shoes. I told her most girls get the dress first, but no, she wanted the shoes." She knew she was rambling, but couldn't seem to stop.

"Gill, take a breath."

"I'm sorry. You don't want to know about the stupid shoes."

"I understand you're upset. We've got about a twenty minute ride. Go ahead now, tell me what happened."

"Marcy may have told you that I called her while Rachel was trying on shoes, and asked about getting us a lunch reservation. She got us one at *Poisson*, and by the time Rachel bought shoes it was nearly noon, so we left there and went right to the restaurant. When we got there, Rachel mentioned that this guy on a scooter seemed to be following us.”

“What?”

“I thought it was just her imagination. We were joking around. She’d seen the same guy outside of Jimmy Choo’s, and when we got to the restaurant we saw him again. She seemed curious about it but I brushed her off. I figured she was just being goofy, like I get sometimes around you, making a mystery out of everything. We laughed about it.”

“What did this guy look like?”

“He was young, dark hair, wearing a baseball cap. I think it said Dodgers. He wore a dark blue *Go Navy* T-shirt and a pair of black jeans.”

“He was riding a scooter?”

“Yes. I think he followed us from Jimmy Choo’s.”

“Are you sure about that, Gill? Because if he did, that’s important information.”

“He must have. We thought he might be paparazzi. Ellen was there. She’d just arrived and the front of the restaurant was packed with photographers. The guy on the scooter whizzed right past us and pulled up in front of our limo.” She chewed on the inside of her cheek. “Damn, I can’t believe I never got Rachel’s cell phone number!”

"It wouldn't have mattered because she's not answering. Marcy's been calling her and the phone goes right to voicemail."

"Oh, no. Kelly, what if something's happened to her and it's all my fault?"

"That's not going to help, Gilly, you know that. As far as we can tell, Rachel's simply gotten herself lost, and Marcy said her phone is likely dead. She's always forgetting to charge it and with all the excitement that's probably what's happened. Now tell me about the scooter guy."

"It was nothing, not really. We had lunch and were getting ready to leave when Ellen and her party got up and started out the door. Of course that caused a big commotion and Rachel got a real kick out of it. We were standing on the steps waiting for everything to clear and watching all the paparazzi swoop down on Ellen's limo. It was parked just a couple of cars ahead of ours. Then I noticed *our* driver standing in front of our limo and the scooter guy was in front of him, yelling and waving his arms. I told Rachel to wait for me on the steps and I went over to see what all the commotion was about."

"What did you find out?"

"The idiot had a dent on the back fender of his scooter and he claimed our limo driver had done it. It was obviously a blatant lie, the dent was so old it was already rusty, but you could tell he intended to make a big scene. I didn't want that to happen, so I gave the guy a hundred dollars and told him to get the hell out of there before I decked him myself. I was pretty steamed, but I didn't want to spoil things for Rachel."

"Did you notice if she was still there while this was going on?"

"She was when we first started talking, but after I'd given the guy the money, I looked back and she wasn't in sight. I wasn't worried at first. I figured she had to go to the bathroom and went back inside. I told the driver to wait and I returned to the restaurant, but no one had seen her and she wasn't in the ladies room. That's when I started to worry and sent you the voicemail."

"Why didn't you text me?"

"Like I said, I wasn't that worried at first. I figured she'd decided to look into another of the shops while I was dealing with the mess and she got distracted. I didn't want to interrupt your meetings but I wanted to get her number so if I didn't find her right away I could call her."

"Okay. Here's what I want you to do. We're only about fifteen minutes away from you now. Go back inside the restaurant and see if you can find anyone who remembers seeing Rachel after you left. Don't go anywhere else. Have the limo driver stay right there and wait for us, but while you're waiting maybe you can line up anyone who might have seen her."

"Okay. And Kelly," Gillian sniffled his name. "Please hurry."

"I will, sweetheart. Don't worry. Everything's going to be okay."

Chapter Four

Kelly and Marcy's driver pulled his black limousine up behind Gillian's on the street in front of *Poisson*. Kelly jumped out the minute the car stopped and met Gillian on the sidewalk. Her face was red and he knew it wasn't from the warm temperatures.

He pulled her into his arms and squeezed, then pressed a kiss to her temple. "Any sign of Rachel?"

"No. She's just vanished. Nobody's seen her and nobody remembers anything." Gillian dissolved into sobs.

Kelly held her tight, rubbing his hand over her back. "Shhh. We'll find her.'

Marcy joined them on the sidewalk. "I've left messages on her phone. She's always forgetting to charge the stupid thing so getting her voicemail doesn't surprise me. What does is the fact that she hasn't tried to call me. She's a smart girl. She knows you'd be worried and that I'd be frantic once I learned she'd taken off. It's just not like her." Marcy's normally soft voice showed signs of panic.

"That's what I've been worrying about."
Gillian reached for Marcy's hand. "She was
right there on the step. I didn't want to get
her into the middle of whatever was going
on with the driver, so I told her to wait *right
there.*"

"This is *not* your fault Gillian." Marcy
gripped her hand harder. "I don't know
what happened, but whatever it was, it
wasn't anything you did. If I'd been with her
I'd have done exactly the same thing. You
don't drag a young girl into what could
possibly be a fight between two men."

Gillian nodded. "I keep going over and
over everything in my mind. When I first
reached the driver and scooter guy, I looked
back at Rachel and she was just standing on
the step with her eyes glued to Ellen and her
entourage. When I looked again, just a few
minutes later, she wasn't there."

"Maybe we should call the police?"
Marcy looked to Kelly to see if he agreed.

He scratched his chin. "Not sure there'd
be much point. They won't do anything
until twenty-four to forty-eight hours have
passed, and even then, this is Beverly Hills.
I can imagine how many young girls come
to LA and the Hollywood area and
disappear voluntarily."

"Rachel would never do that."

"I know she wouldn't, Marcy. I don't
mean to imply that she would. What I mean
is, the police don't know us and they don't
know Rachel. They get dozens of calls like

this every day, so they're not going to pay us much attention. But I'll talk to them." He raised his brows and shrugged. "On the other hand, we might as well play the celebrity card. They could pay more attention when they find out she's Marcy's sister."

"So let's go!" Marcy fidgeted impatiently. Her face was pale and Kelly didn't think she looked well.

He shook his head. "Uh, no. The last thing I need to do is drag you into a police station. Your publicist would have my hide. You two are going back to the hotel."

"Who cares what he says? This is my *sister*, Kelly!"

"We can't just leave her out there!" Gillian squeezed Kelly's arm.

"We're not going to. I've got a friend who works for one of the big PI firms out here. I'm gonna get him on the phone and have a little chat. Then I'll head to the local PD. Between all of us, we're gonna cover every inch of Beverly Hills until we find that girl."

Gillian looked like she was going to protest.

Kelly squeezed her hand. "I need you to work with me, here. Go on back to the hotel and wait in Marcy's suite. There's a possibility Rachel could return and you should be there if she does."

Marcy looked ready to burst into tears. "But shouldn't we help you search for her?"

"Right now I just want the two of you safe. I've got things to do, and I can't be worrying about you, too. Lenny, our driver, is an off duty cop. I'm going to ask him to take you back and stay with you until I return. "

"Kelly's right. We need to look after you." Gillian was still holding Marcy's hand. "We'll go back to the hotel and let them know at the front desk that we're looking for Rachel. Maybe someone there will have seen her. It's possible something happened that caused Rachel to go back by herself. We might be really surprised and find her waiting in your suite."

Kelly could tell by the expression on his wife's face that the explanation sounded lame even to her, but he appreciated her trying to keep the other girl calm.

Marcy nodded and looked at him. "You'll call and let us know what's going on?"

"Of course I will. I'll keep in touch with you. Don't worry. There's an explanation for this, and just because we don't know what it is, doesn't mean something awful has happened. We're going to find that little gal and then we're all going out to dinner with Blake Shelton. We can regale him with the story of our scary first day in Beverly Hills." He placed a hand on Marcy's shoulder and squeezed, hoping he was reassuring her. She really didn't look well.

Kelly pressed one more kiss to Gillian's temple before ushering them both into the back of his car. Leaning in to the driver he said, "Lenny, take these girls back to the hotel and stay with them, will you please? I'm going to rent a car and head over to the local police department."

The muscular, bald black man gazed at him. "Why rent a car? Let Smokey take you." He motioned to Gillian and Rachel's limo. "He knows the area, you don't."

Kelly scratched his chin. "Feel damn silly arriving at the PD in a limo."

Lenny lowered his head and peered over the tops of his sunglasses. "Who gives a shit about 'silly'? You and I both know time is of the essence in a case like this. It'll take you an hour to rent a car and figure out where you need to go. Smoky can have you there in ten minutes. Go with what you got, brother."

"You're right. I'll use the time to call my PI friend, Stan." He lowered his voice. "I need all the help I can get on this thing."

"If there's anything I can do, you just have to ask."

"Thanks, man." He nodded toward the back of the car. "Keeping an eye on these two is all I need just now. Appreciate it, though." He stood and patted the roof of the car, then watched as Lenny drove off.

He'd tried to be strong for Marcy and Gillian, but he didn't like this situation one bit. Rachel was young, pretty, and not accustomed to a city like this one. A multitude of things could have happened, and not one of the possibilities in his mind was good.

As Smokey drove the limo through town, Kelly called Gus to fill him in. His second call was to his old PI friend, Stan Mason. He and Stan worked together a few times in Fort Worth, before the other man had followed the woman of his dreams to the west coast.

"Mason," he answered on the second ring.

"Well, if it isn't the only man I know who drinks cheap scotch because he likes the taste of it."

"Kelly McWinter, you old dog, you! That was a cover story, you know. I drank cheap scotch because that's what I could afford, but who wants to admit that?"

Kelly chuckled. "Hey, Stan, how are you? How's—what was her name—Shaniqua?"

"I'm fine. Shaniqua is great, living the good life in Beverly Hills. We had a kid last year. Trevor's almost one and a half now."

"A kid? Holy smokes, man! How's that going?"

"Couldn't be better. Lives with his mom half the week and me the rest of the time."

Kelly hesitated. "O-kay. I thought you said Shaniqua was great, living the good life."

Stan chuckled. "She is, on my alimony and child support. That's how she can afford the good life."

Kelly shook his head. "Shit. Sorry, buddy. I didn't know."

"Yeah, well it's not the kind of news you write home about. And I would have come back to Texas, except for Trevor. My old man was an absentee father. I won't be that kind of dad to my kid."

"Good for you. Sounds like the right call."

"Speaking of calls, what the hell is up? You in town, or still in the backwoods swamps of Indian Creek?"

Kelly cleared his throat. "We have indoor plumbing now, and fewer swamps. But yeah, I'm in town on a security detail. My client is Marcy Fischer, the country music singer."

"I've heard of her! Pretty little thing, good voice."

"She's up for the female vocalist of the year at the CMA awards, so she's doing all right. But listen, she's here with her younger sister. Rachel is twenty-one, a college student at Nashville State." He told Stan the condensed version of what had happened.

"Damn, man, that doesn't sound good. You going to the police or are you looking for some help from me?"

"Both. I'm not sure how much they'll be willing to do this early, but I can't just sit on

76

my hands here. Her sister—not to mention *my wife*—will have my hide if I don't get this resolved quickly."

"Let's meet at the Beverly Hills PD, you know where that is?"

"I have a driver."

"Good. I'll meet you out front in—" he hesitated. "Twenty minutes?"

Kelly moved his phone aside and said to Smokey, "Can we be at the Beverly Hills PD in twenty minutes?"

"More like ten," the driver replied.

Speaking into his phone Kelly confirmed, "No problem. See you then. And, Stan? Thanks."

"Happy to help an old friend. See you soon." He ended the call.

Kelly pocketed his phone and leaned back, glancing out the windows. The scenery was picture-postcard perfect. *Too damn bad things always have to go south. Whenever life starts to feel like everything is falling into place, something always happens to spoil it.*

He sighed. Some days he felt like bad luck followed him, from the untimely and tragic death of his first wife, to a series of losses he'd suffered over the past few years. He knew it was the same for everybody, *shit happens*, but often he wondered if he saw more of it because of the nature of his job. He'd been a cop for years before he became a PI. He'd seen a lot in those years. Things were much better now. Still, shit continued to happen. He sighed again, thinking about the turn his honeymoon had taken.

Damned if I couldn't stand to be happy for more than a few days at a time.

He checked his watch and decided the girls had had enough time to get back to the Wilshire. He dialed Gillian's cell and listened as it rang.

"Hey, sugar," she answered.

"Hi babe. Any news there?"

"No. Not a word."

"Say, do you have a picture of Rachel on your phone? I meant to ask Marcy."

"I do. I'll send it to you."

"Good, thanks."

"Sure. I finally convinced Marcy to take a nap. Last time I checked she'd actually fallen asleep and I'm hoping she stays that way. Did you know she's two months pregnant?"

"You're kidding, right?"

"I'm not. They've been keeping it a secret because of the child she lost."

"Makes sense. That's probably one of the reason's Mark was so determined I go with her."

"They were both really broken up when she lost Alex Wyatt's baby. Wyatt was a slimeball, but Marcy and Mark both considered that baby to be their own. Frankly, I was happy Wyatt was out of the picture and they wouldn't have to deal with any co-parenting issues. All water under the bridge now. I kinda figured the months she spent in jail probably contributed to her miscarriage.”

“You never know, they could have.”

Gillian sighed. “So you understand how hesitant they are now. They don’t want anyone to know until she’s well into her second trimester. Mark really didn’t want Marcy to attend these awards, but her doctor gave her clearance and she wanted to come so he relented, provided you agreed.”

“I knew that part, but he didn’t tell me about the pregnancy. It stands to reason Rachel’s disappearance has knocked her off balance.”

Gillian frowned. “She looked so pale when we got to the room, and I wanted to call in the hotel’s doctor. That’s when she broke down and told me about the baby. It turns out she’s been dealing with morning sickness, which partially accounts for her pallor. She asked me not to tell anyone but you–she knew I’d do that–and she promised to try and get some rest. She needs to keep her strength up for the baby.”

“I can understand why she didn’t want to call a hotel doctor. In this town that’d be the same as posting her pregnancy on Twitter. Pretty well everyone who comes in contact with celebrities in this town has a direct pipeline to the tabloids.”

“That’s what she said. I’ll keep a close eye on her. Tabloids or not, if she continues to look like she’s in trouble, I’m calling someone.”

"Agreed. Thanks for taking care of her, Gill."

His wife snorted. "Yeah, like I did such a good job with her sister!"

"Gilly, don't. You didn't do anything wrong. It's rotten that Rachel's been taken, but nothing you did or didn't do would have changed things. They wanted Rachel and they grabbed her. I'm just thankful they didn't get you too. Now, I've got to go. We're pulling up to the police department but I'll call again when I'm done. Love you."

"I love you too, honey." She ended the call.

Kelly hated hearing the tone of her voice. He needed to find Rachel *pronto*.

Smokey maneuvered his longer than normal car into a parking spot across the street from the Beverly Hills PD on Palisades Drive.

Kelly studied the white brick building framed by groups of palm trees. California had such a different feel about it. He hadn't quite decided if he liked it or not.

A white convertible parked close to them and when the driver climbed out, Kelly recognized Stan. "Not sure how long this will take," he told Smokey.

"I'll be right here." The driver took out his cell phone and began scrolling through it.

Chuckling as he approached Stan, he marveled at how far technology had come. With access to a smart phone, waiting was no longer the boring affair it used to be. The internet offered a wealth of opportunities for time killers. "Hey!" He quickened his pace to catch up to Stan.

The tall, lanky man paused and turned around. "Kelly! How the heck are ya?" He pumped Kelly's hand enthusiastically.

"Fine. Just fine."

"Did I hear you mention a wife?"

He smiled and nodded. "I did. Her name's Gillian."

"I'd like to meet her."

"Hopefully we can find Rachel and make that happen. The clock is ticking here, Stan, and I gotta admit I'm worried."

"Let's go in. I called ahead and we'll be meeting with a detective friend of mine, Dave Harrison."

"Good deal." They entered the building.

After going through the requisite front desk check in and identification, Kelly and Stan were directed to a room with a couple of comfortable chairs, a counter with a Keurig set up for coffee and tea, and a small writing table. In the corner a lemon tree grew out of a cedar chip lined square reaching toward an overhead skylight. Kelly chuckled. *Damn, I need to have a word with Gus about giving the FWPD a facelift.* Still smiling, he pushed the button on the Keurig to fill his coffee cup.

"Either you really like our coffee or something in here's struck your funny bone."

He turned around to face the speaker, a tall, well-built guy with black hair and eyes, set off by an immaculate navy blue suit, white shirt and matching tie.

Kelly wasn't sure he could explain the differences in their police departments so he decided to let it drop. "Good coffee."

Stan held out his hand and received a firm shake in response. "Hey, Dave. Thanks for meeting us. This is the PI from Texas I was telling you about, Kelly McWinter."

Dave turned to Kelly and extended a hand. "Dave Harrison. I've already talked with a Chief Graham in Fort Worth. He spoke very highly of you and asked me to give you every courtesy. But I'm still curious as to what you found so funny. That was almost a belly laugh you had going when I opened the door."

Kelly grinned. "You'd have to know the chief. Augustus Graham is known as Gus to those of us who've been around long enough to brave familiarity, but he's the genuine article. Anyway, I was checking out the cushy chairs, the fancy Keurig, and the tree growing to the skylight. It occurred to me I'd have to speak to Gus about upgrading the facilities downtown a bit."

Dave's smile had appeared the minute Kelly launched into his description of Gus. By the time Kelly finished describing his thoughts on the upgrades, Dave had a full-out grin going. "I transferred over here from Wilshire, and I've worked with a few chiefs like yours. Me, I'm just a couple years shy of retirement so the perks here suit me just fine. But still, I'd sure like to be a fly on the wall when you make your recommendations back home."

"Yeah. Might have to wait awhile for that. This ol' boy's mama didn't raise no fool."

Still smiling, Dave motioned for Kelly and Stan to take seats. "I understand you're looking for a young girl that seems to have disappeared somewhere along Rodeo Drive." Dave fixed himself a coffee and joined them.

"That's right. Rachel Benson. She's Marcy Fischer's younger sister. At this point we don't have any reason to suspect foul play, but my gut tells me this is more than just a girl wandering off on her own."

Dave frowned, and then turned to write on his notepad. "You understand, I have to ask, is it possible this girl might have taken off on her own? We get a lot of that here. You'd be surprised how star struck some of these youngsters can get."

Kelly nodded. "I know that Dave, and if I had even a glimmer of suspicion she might have done that I wouldn't be taking up your time. The thing is, Marcy's had some trouble with an over-zealous fan. In fact, a couple months ago this guy actually broke into her house and made it all the way upstairs to the master bedroom before Marcy's dog took him down. Rachel would never put her sister through that kind of stress. She's not the type." Kelly leaned forward and held out his phone. "This is Marcy with her sister Rachel. The little blonde is the one that's missing."

"Damn shame. Pretty girls, both of them."

"I know, and I think they're smart too. Rachel grew up around Marcy's fame. She knows how to take care of herself. She wouldn't just wander off, or go with a stranger, and she'd never leave her sister to worry about what had happened to her. Marcy's husband Mark is overseas and the entire family worried about Marcy coming to California by herself. Matter of fact, if I hadn't agreed to bring my wife and come along on this trip, Marcy had already promised Mark she'd give up the chance of attending the awards all together."

"Can I send this picture to my phone so I can print it off? The girl looks kind of familiar, but I can't think why."

"Please do." Kelly handed his cell over and Dave texted himself.

He handed it back, and Kelly pocketed it. "I know you can't do anything officially – it's only been a few hours, but I'd be mighty grateful if you'd do whatever you can. Maybe pass that around amongst the patrolmen and get them to be on the lookout."

"Be glad to help. I'll alert the guys at LAPD as well. We've always gotten support whenever we've asked for it from our brothers in Texas. You can count on us for anything we can do here."

"Thanks. I appreciate that a lot. Stan has agreed to help out as well."

The other PI nodded. "I've got half a dozen people ready to hit the streets when we get them that photo. Each of them has a group of confidential informants, so we can cast a pretty big net here in the next couple of hours."

Dave sipped his coffee. "Good deal. Finding a missing girl is hard as hell in the middle of a tourist destination like Beverly Hills. We've got to put as many resources on it as fast as we can. Let me get a few more details. For the time being I'll put out a BOLO. Hopefully we won't need a missing persons report, but that can't happen for forty-eight hours. Just remember, if this takes a turn outside the law, you need to get me on the horn fast. You've got my cell number in your phone now. Agreed?"

Kelly couldn't have agreed more whole-heartedly. "Damn straight. I appreciate the support you're offering and you've got my word. If this turns out to be anything more than just a young girl getting lost and being too embarrassed to call for help, you'll be the first person I call. Nothing I'd like better than to give y'all a call and apologize for takin' your time."

He filled out a report for the detective while Stan texted Rachel's photo to his operatives. He immediately got a text back.

Is that Lacey Bettman?

Stan glanced up from his phone. "Who the hell is Lacey Bettman?"

Dave snapped his fingers. "That's who the photo reminded me of! She's a young actress from one of those reality shows. You know the type, rich father, spoiled daughter. Carries a ten-cent dog in her pocketbook. That kind."

Kelly exchanged glances with Dave then Stan. "Do we think this means something?"

"Interesting detail," Stan mused.

Dave asked, "Did you speak with the staff at *Poisson*? Anybody see anything unusual?"

Guilt crept over Kelly. "My wife spoke with them. She'd just had lunch there with Rachel." *Damn it!* He'd known Gill's state of mind. He should never have put that burden on her. "I'm thinking I need to go back there and talk to them myself."

Dave nodded. "The manager of the restaurant is a guy named Chen Li. Don't worry, he's Asian but speaks perfect English. Tell him I sent you. That might pave the way for his cooperation."

"Thank you." Kelly rose and the others followed suit.

"Keep me posted," Dave said.

"Will do." Kelly shook his hand, then Stan did, and while Dave exited through a back door, they went out through the front.

"I'm going to hit the streets. I'll stay in touch." Stan climbed into his car.

"Sounds good. Thanks again." Kelly slid into the back seat of the limo. "Hey, Smokey. We're headed back to the restaurant, please."

"You got it, Mr. McWinter." He pulled out onto the street.

Kelly called Gillian's cell phone again.

"Any news?" she answered.

"Not yet, but we've got a lot of people beating the pavement now. The police have put out a 'be on the lookout' alert. I'm headed back to the restaurant to speak with the manager."

"Oh. I didn't think of talking to him."

"It's fine, Gill. I should have done it while I was there the first time."

"Everything happened so fast."

"I'm a bit off my game. This one is hitting a little too close to home for my comfort level. I hate putting you in the middle of any of my cases."

"I'm a big girl, Kelly. Not some fragile china doll."

"Never said you were, sugar. I just want to keep you safe is all."

"I'm safe, babe. Marcy's your client, remember?"

"That's just it. *Marcy's a client.* You're my life, Gillian McWinter. I'd go to hell and back for my clients, but there's nothing I wouldn't do to protect you."

"Aw, you know how to choke a girl up, don't you? Be safe out there, husband. I need you, too. And I love you more than I ever dreamed was possible."

He smiled. "You too, sweet thing. Talk to you soon."

"Kelly, wait! What about Blake and dinner?"

He rubbed his temple with his free hand. "I hate to say this, but I think I better give him a call and see if we can't reschedule. I know you were looking forward to meeting him, but I doubt Marcy or Rachel – when we find her – are going to feel much like an evening out on the town."

"I completely agree. As much as I wanted to meet Blake Shelton, I can't imagine going out after what we've been through today."

"Another time," he agreed.

"You bet. Go on now, and find her."

"I intend to. Thanks." Kelly punched the talk button off and tossed his phone on the seat. He rubbed both temples now, kicking himself for the mental mistakes he'd already made. He sincerely hoped Rachel didn't pay the price for his oversights.

Chapter Five

Back at Poisson, Kelly asked the hostess for the restaurant manager, Chen Li, and was shown to a spacious office in the rear of the building.

"May I help you?" A sharply dressed Asian man stepped out from behind the desk with his hand extended in greeting.

"Yes. I appreciate you seeing me, Mr. Li." Kelly shook hands and accepted a chair when Li indicated he should sit. "I'm Kelly McWinter, a private investigator from Fort Worth, Texas. Dave Harrison over at the police department suggested I speak with you."

Li nodded and took his seat. "Is this concerning the young woman who went missing this afternoon? I'd hoped she would have turned up by now."

"Me too. I was in town protecting her sister when this happened. I realize my wife has spoken with some of your employees, but I need to question anyone who was here just one more time if I might, please."

"Of course. We are terribly sorry about the whole incident. I have personally spoken with all of our employees and one of them, Vicky Madison, believes she might have seen your missing woman speaking to a man out on the front steps."

"That's excellent news, Mr. Li. Is it possible for me to speak with Miss Madison?"

"Most definitely. I must go to the kitchen to supervise the dinner preparations, but I'll send Vicky right in."

Kelly rose. "I can't thank you enough for your help." The two shook hands and Li left the office.

A few minutes later, a short brunette with nervous eyes entered the office and looked hesitantly at Kelly.

"Miss Madison." He stood and smiled in welcome.

"Vicky, please. Mr. Li said you wanted to speak with me?"

"Please, sit." Kelly settled back into one of the leather chairs and indicated Vicky should take the other.

"Thank you. I don't know if I can be much help, but I did recognize the girl Mr. Li said was missing. She came into the restaurant during the lunch rush, with another blonde woman. They were seated in the main dining room. The reason I noticed them particularly is because the girl was a dead ringer for one of the celebrity clients I was looking after in a private room."

Kelly blinked. "That's what I understand, but I didn't know the actress was here. Rachel's family and I will be extremely grateful for any details you can share."

"Well it's not a lot. Just that your girl, Rachel, looks exactly like Lacey Bettman, the reality star. Madeline, one of the main room's waitresses, and I were both picking up orders when she pointed to the two women sitting in her station and asked if I didn't think the younger girl looked exactly like Lacey. I couldn't believe it. She was a dead ringer."

"And this was about what time?"

"It was noon. The rush was in full swing and I only had a minute to chat with Madeline, but she was right. The resemblance was uncanny."

"Was that the last you saw of the young woman and her companion?"

"No. After lunch, Lacey and her gentleman friend slipped out the back door, avoiding the paparazzi, you know. After I cleaned their room I headed up front and noticed that Ellen was just leaving the restaurant. She always causes a stir whenever she comes and goes, so I went over and stood beside the front windows and watched the activity outside."

"Did you see Rachel at that time?"

"Not right away, but once Ellen and all the paparazzi moved down toward her limo, I spotted your girl standing on the steps of the restaurant watching them. Like I said, the resemblance between her and Lacey is so striking that I was drawn to watch her."

"Was she alone?"

"She was at first. She seemed to be watching her companion who was on the sidewalk talking to a limo driver and some kid on a motor scooter. There was a bit of a confrontation going on."

"Rachel stayed on the steps alone?"

"I watched the others for a few minutes and then, when I glanced back at the girl she was walking down the steps with a man. He seemed to be helping her, like she was ill or something. He had his arm around her waist and she was kind of stumbling. To be honest, I thought maybe that was her boyfriend, and she'd had too much to drink at lunch. Anyway, right then, Mr. Li called me and I went back to work. I'm afraid that's all I know."

"Can you describe the man at all? Height in comparison to Rachel, hair color, clothes?"

"He was taller than her, I'd say maybe six foot. Thick black hair, big chested. He was wearing jeans and a black shirt."

"That's good. Anything else you noticed?"

She thought for a moment, and then shook her head.

"Did you see where they went? What he might have been driving?"

"There was a black minivan parked in the delivery zone. I noticed it because no one is supposed to park there, and I told Mr. Li about it. He went out to check, but it was gone. I guess it might have belonged to the man. I really couldn't say."

"I don't suppose you noticed the model or the license number?"

"No, sorry. I didn't pay much attention other than to think I'd better tell Mr. Li."

Kelly stood. "You've been a big help, Vicky. Thanks for speaking with me. I'm going to head out, see if anyone else might have noticed anything."

She nodded and rose. "Right this way."

He followed her out and spoke with the rest of the staff. Most had just come on duty, and the ones who'd been there for lunch said they hadn't noticed Rachel. With more thanks to Mr. Li, Kelly headed back to the Beverly Hills precinct.

He texted Dave and when he arrived, was shown into his office.

"I might have a break." Kelly shook hands with Dave and took a seat across from the desk. "If I'm right, you're going to want to be in on this."

"You've got my attention. Shoot."

Kelly outlined everything he'd discovered during his conversation with Vicky and his own speculation that Lacey Bettman might have been the intended target for what he was now fairly certain had been an abduction.

"Hand me the descriptions you've got on the guy and the van." Dave stood and reached for Kelly's notebook."

"It's all there."

"Good. Let's go to the media room and see if we can spot the van. We've got cameras all along Rodeo Drive, shouldn't be that hard to pick it out."

For thirty minutes they watched hundreds of images flashing past on an entire bank of screens when Kelly lifted his hand to point at a screen. "There."

Dave called the technician monitoring the screens. "Freeze that one."

It showed a dark blue van pull up to the front of Poisson and then carefully pull into the curb and back up until the vehicle was nearly hidden behind a flowering Silk Floss. The tree, in full bloom and loaded with deep pink blossoms, formed a perfect screen for the van, practically hiding it from the eye of anyone standing on the front steps of the restaurant.

"I'll be damned." Dave shook his head and walked over to the technician. "Riley, can you zoom in on the license plate and get the number?"

The uniformed man nodded. "Should be able to, give me a few minutes."

Dave walked back to stand beside Kelly while Riley worked his magic. He looked at Kelly. "You understand we don't have any reason to question the owner of this vehicle."

"Of course. That's where I come in. I'm not official, and I'm wondering if this guy happened to spot my missing friend. Don't worry, we'll be careful and keep everything above board."

Dave started to speak but Kelly continued, "I know, you want a call the second we have anything you can act on."

"You hit the nail on the head. Now let's see what Riley found."

"I got what you needed." The young man handed a note over to Dave. "Ran it through the database. The van belongs to a Vince Martinez. His address puts him in Venice. On one of the canals."

"Thanks. Damn fast work."

Dave took the note and he and Kelly walked back to his office. "I noticed the limo out front. You using a driver?"

"Yep. Wouldn't have it any other way in this city. Country boy like me'd get lost and never find his way back home without one."

Dave laughed. "Yeah, some country boy. Okay, get him to take you to the Venice Canals. He'll have to find a place to park and let you walk in. You'll see when you get over there. Anything comes up, you got my number. Doesn't matter if it's day or night. Call my cell, I'll answer or get right back to you."

"Thanks, Dave. I appreciate all the help."

"No thanks needed. If you're right, and I've got a gut feeling you are, then you've probably saved me from a major headache. You have no idea the kind of mess it'd bring down on our department if a celebrity got snatched out of a local restaurant."

"Yeah, I get where you're coming from. I just hope Rachel's okay and I'll be delighted to leave the whole mess in your hands if I can only pick up my girl and take her back to her sister."

Kelly took his leave of Dave and instructed his driver to head for Venice Beach.

* * *

Rachel pulled herself up until her head and one of her shoulders rested against a brass headboard. Her arms were tied with rope and fastened to one of the posts and some kind of gag filled her mouth. She wiggled around until she found the least uncomfortable position and began to work on the ropes. *No sniveling*, she warned herself. *Back home they'd be laughed outta 4H for these kind of knots.* Keeping an eye on the door, she worked the rope until her left arm came free. Flexing her fingers, she shifted positions.

"Where's the girl?" A man's voice sounded outside her door.

"Sleeping. Don't worry. I gave her enough stuff to keep her out for hours."

"Yeah. I'll see for myself."

Rachel slipped her hand back into the rope and let herself fall sideways on the bed. Eyes closed, breathing deeply, she waited.

96

"See. I told you. Dead to the world."

"Just see that she stays that way."

"What are we supposed to do with her?"

"That's up to Jared. Did she see your face?"

"Nope. She had her back turned when I stuck her and she's been out ever since."

"Put the hood over your face next time you come in here. Jared'll probably let her go once we get the money, but not if she sees our faces."

"Hey, I never signed up for no murder."

"What's the difference? Kidnapping's almost as bad."

Rachel's eyelids lifted just enough to see the men standing at the foot of her bed. Making a mental note of their features, she squeezed her eyelids closed.

"Okay. I'm going back to the club. I'll call as soon as there's news. Keep the girl quiet. If she wakes up give her another shot and put the hood on next time. She's bound to wake up soon."

* * *

At the end of Venice Boulevard Kelly told his driver to pull into a lot where he could park and wait for Kelly's return. Then he crossed the street to a shop advertising souvenirs and gifts. Inside he purchased a bright Hawaiian shirt and a white canvas hat.

97

"I'm kinda overdressed for the beach," he joked with the elderly Asian clerk, "mind if I use your change room to get out of these city clothes?"

Smiling and nodding she directed him to a change room at the back of the store, where he took off his shirt and slid his arms into his gaudy green and yellow purchase. Then, stuffing his clothes into the oversized *Venice Beach* bag he'd just purchased, he plopped the hat on his head and said goodbye to the clerk.

Leaving the store, he walked along the sidewalk until he came to a white rail bridge where he crossed over and ended up on Lincoln Avenue. Another block down he spotted a small tract house crowded between two opulent homes. The house, a striking contrast to the mansions lining the canals, appeared to be a nineteen-sixties holdout from developers and stuck out like a weed in the middle of a manicured lawn.

That's got to be it. Now to get a look inside.

He walked to the door of the small house, pressed the doorbell and pasted his best good ol' boy smile on his face. A minute passed, then two. Kelly pressed his finger on the doorbell again and held it there.

Finally the door opened and a tall, dark skinned man with grease caked hair hanging in his face stuck his head out the door.

"What do ya' want?" The man's scowl wasn't altered by Kelly's friendly smile.

"Oh hi there. Sorry to bother you," Kelly stuck out his hand.

The man ignored it. "We ain't buying anything."

Kelly laughed. "Oh no. I'm no salesman. Actually I'm a potential customer. I couldn't help but notice this house was, shall we say, not quite up to the neighborhood." Kelly chuckled again, and the guy in the doorway kept scowling.

"We're from Nebraska. I'm thinking of retiring out here, and yesterday when we went on a tour of this area, my wife she just plumb fell in love with these canals. Can't get it out of her head that we can't afford to live around here. I came back to walk around the neighborhood, and that's when I spotted this place."

The guy in the door leaned forward. "We ain't interested. This place ain't for sale." He slammed the door.

Kelly stepped quickly back then dropped his shoulders dejectedly. He returned to the walkway and back to the sidewalk.

Once out of sight, he reached for his cell and called the detective's number.

"We've got the right place." Kelly spoke as soon as Dave's voice came on the line. "I spotted Rachel's bag sitting on the floor beside the couch. That's all I needed to know she's in there, and I think the guy who's got her is in there by himself. I didn't hear any other noises in the house and I'd have felt it if there'd been movement."

"Do you think he made you?"

"Not a chance. First of all, the guy's dumb as a rock and second he listened to my spiel too long for someone spooked. He's probably just the babysitter, and he was both bored and stupid."

"Okay. You hang back. We'll be there in ten minutes. You will wait for us.?"

The question was more of a command. Kelly smiled. "You got it."

* * *

Inside the house, Rachel finished freeing herself from the rope, slid off the bed and tiptoed to the door. Turning the handle carefully, she listened to voices and finally identified the voice of Rob Wells from *Trailer Park Boys*. Relieved that her captor seemed to be engrossed in a TV show, Rachel opened the door just wide enough to slide through. Finding herself in what seemed to be a hallway leading to the living room on the left and the kitchen and back of the house on the right, she pressed herself against the wall and moved slowly to the right until she spotted an outside back door, open and facing out onto what looked like some kind of small waterway. She unlatched the screen and took a step onto the back porch.

A hand covered her mouth and a man's arm pulled her back against his rock-hard chest. His grip was so tight she couldn't move. She tried to scream but he muttered into her ear,

"Don't make a sound."

* * *

Patience had never been Kelly's strongest suit. He could sit on a stakeout for as long as necessary, but waiting for the cops to arrive so he could rescue someone he was supposed to be watching out for nearly drove him over the edge. When he spotted Dave in an unmarked car, followed closely by two black and whites, his heart skipped into overdrive and his reflexes tensed to full alert.

The police parked, and half a dozen officers joined him, slipping into Kevlar vests.

"Did you actually see Rachel?" Dave asked Kelly as he strapped his vest on. He handed an extra vest over.

"Thanks." Kelly geared up. "No, I didn't, just her bag. There was a hallway leading off the front room. I'm guessing she's back there."

Nodding, Dave motioned the officers forward and they advanced quietly. He shot Kelly a look. "Hang back, you hear?"

"Ten-four."

* * *

Rachel struggled to get free.

"Don't panic. I'm a police officer," the man whispered into her ear.

Rachel nodded her head and stopped resisting. She let her body go limp.

"Don't say a word."

She nodded again.

He released the hand from her mouth. "Can you walk?"

"Yes."

Motioning to the sidewalk he said, "Go out the back gate. There's an officer waiting, she'll take you to Mr. McWinter."

"Thank you so much." Rachel gave the officer a quick hug then hurried down the walkway. She opened the gate and ran straight into the arms of a sturdy black woman with a warm smile and big solid arms. The uniformed woman slid an arm around her shoulders and led her down the path toward a bridge where Kelly waited.

She'd never been so happy to see anyone in her life.

The expression on his face reflected the same feelings.

When she got to within a couple feet of Kelly she broke free from the woman and raced toward him.

He jogged to meet her and scooped her into his arms. "Holy guacamole, kiddo. Am I ever glad to see you."

Rachel felt truly safe for the first time in hours. She rested her head against his chest for a minute, then pulled back and grinned. "I got away, Kelly. Slipped out of the ropes and was headed out the back door when the cops showed up!"

He chuckled. "Those bozos didn't know who they were messing with. Good job, Rachel." Pulling his cell from his pocket, he punched Gillian's number, still smiling.

"Kelly?" His wife's voice was breathy.

"Hey, sugar. You wanna put Marcy on the phone? I've got someone here who's real anxious to say hello."

Chapter Six

The private jet sped down the runway of Los Angeles International airport and with a surge of speed, soared into the sky. Kelly glanced across the aisle at the sisters who'd been inseparable since he'd returned Rachel to the hotel.

"Thank God that's over." Marcy squeezed Rachel's hand. "I feel as if I've been holding my breath ever since Kelly brought you back. I couldn't shake the feeling I was going to lose you again."

"Okay, big sister, enough of that. I'm fine. It was scary, sure, but actually I feel pretty good about outsmarting those clowns." Rachel laughed out loud.

Kelly exchanged amused glances with Gillian.

Marcy stifled a sob. "You do know they could have killed you and dumped your body in the ocean."

Rachel, realizing her sister was genuinely upset, stopped laughing and squeezed Marcy's hand. "I'm sorry, Sis. Please don't cry. It's not good for you know who."

"It's okay." Marcy wiped her eyes. "You don't have to keep quiet about the baby. I've told Gillian and I'm sure she's already told Kelly."

"Guilty." Gillian joined the conversation. "I figured it would be okay. I was too excited to keep it from him and anyway, he needs to know so he can be extra careful to keep you safe."

"Of course it's okay, and I'm going to be just fine. I already feel better just leaving that city behind. I know it's probably silly and there are lots of wonderful people in LA, but after what happened to Rachel I'll never feel safe there again."

Kelly nodded. "It's understandable. Just as long as you remember everything's fine now. We're on our way to Las Vegas and I hope you won't let what happened spoil your excitement over the award that I'm darn sure you're going to be packing home."

"Thanks Kelly. That's sweet of you. I really am looking forward to the awards ceremony, but I probably won't feel completely easy until we are all safely back home again."

"That's only natural, but remember Rachel wasn't actually the target of those bozos. It was all a case of bad timing and dumb criminals. Even so, we still have to stay alert. Your safety is our priority, and it's important that we don't let down our guard now that we've left that mess in California behind us."

"Sometimes I hate the fact that I'm never allowed to just go places and do things like everyone else without always having to worry about who might recognize me and what their intentions might be."

"That's the downside of celebrity." Kelly nodded his agreement. "Especially when you're out in the mainstream. Not that this kind of thing couldn't happen in Texas, or even at your home in Nashville, which you well know, but somehow or other there's more of a perception of personal safety when you're down South than when you're out here on the West coast."

"I know, and you have no idea how grateful I am that you and Gillian came with us. I get chills up my backbone when I think about what might have happened to Rachel if you hadn't been along."

"Don't think about it, let's just get your mind on winning that award."

"I know what I'm thinking about." Gillian chimed in. "You haven't told us what you're planning to wear. Is it a secret or will you share?"

"Oh, I haven't even thought about my dress the last couple of days. I meant to show it to you and Rachel last night and then everything happened." For a minute her lip trembled, but she pulled herself up and smiled at Gillian. "I used a local designer, Marie Sampson, she does most of her work by hand, and her gowns are gorgeous. It's pale yellow, strapless, with a form fitting bodice and the skirt is embroidered with climbing roses and silver threads. It flares out from the waist into a kind of bouffant ruffle that reaches just above the knee in front and drops until it almost reaches the floor in back."

"It sounds divine."

Marcy smiled. "Another month and it won't fit." She touched her stomach thoughtfully.

"What about shoes?" Rachel spoke up. "You didn't get a chance to go shopping."

Marcy shook her head and laughed. "Talk about priorities. You seem a lot more upset about me not getting shoes than about you getting kidnapped."

"Never mind that." Rachel waved away concern about herself. "What are you going to do about shoes? I think mine are too big for you. Maybe we can go shopping in Las Vegas?"

"Don't worry. There are some perks to being a celebrity, and I took advantage of one of them while we were waiting for news. I called the studio and they sent a saleswoman from Jimmy Choo's to the suite with shoes and bags. I picked a pair of silver Tilly sandals and a clutch to match the silver threads in the dress."

"They sound fabulous." Gillian commented, and smiled at Kelly who nodded his satisfaction that she'd been able to redirect Marcy's thoughts away from the kidnapping.

The pilot's voice interrupted the fashion discussion. "Time to buckle up. We're starting our descent into Las Vegas."

* * *

"I hope you don't mind the change in accommodations." Kelly escorted Marcy and Rachel into the private elevator and pressed the button for the Presidential suite, where, within minutes they exited directly into the suite atop Harrah's Las Vegas.

"It's perfect. Frankly I'm grateful for a bit of distance from all the fuss and furor that's bound to be going on over at the MGM Grand."

"Good. Then you won't mind if I leave you and Rachel here while I escort Gillian on over to the Grand and we take possession of your suite."

"We'll be just fine. We can spend the afternoon reminiscing and catching up on each other's lives. It'll be like being at school again."

"That's good. I need to get Gillian over there and make sure that everyone knows she's your personal assistant and will be handling everything for you while you are in Las Vegas. We're letting the hotel know that you have your own staff and anything that requires attention will be handled directly through Gillian."

"Sounds organized. Will Rachel be staying here with me?"

"She'll stay here all afternoon. We'll be giving everyone the word that you and Rachel have gone shopping together and will arrive at the hotel later. When it's time for both of you to dress for dinner, the limo driver will pick you up and take you to the MGM Grand. I'll be downstairs waiting for you to arrive and we'll be certain that you make a grand entrance, loaded down with an appropriate number of shopping bags, which I'm having the driver procure this afternoon."

"It all sounds very complicated."

"Nothing to worry about. Everyone will know their parts. All you have to do is relax and enjoy the afternoon with Rachel. Then once you join us at the MGM you can concentrate on getting ready for the awards. Have you written your speech?"

"Oh my gosh, I'm not that confident. To tell you the truth, I haven't even thought about it. There are lots of good singers up for the award, and if I do happen to be lucky enough to win, I guess I'll just speak from the heart."

"Those are always the best speeches. The prepared ones sound phony and nobody listens anyhow."

"What about my night clothes? I'll need something to change into when I come back here after the awards."

"If you and Gillian want to go into the bedroom, I've had the attendant lay out your cases so you can pick out whatever you want to keep here and put it in the dresser. The rest of your clothing, including your formal wear for the evening, Gillian will unpack and have ready for you over at the MGM."

"What about Rachel's things?"

"If she needs anything for the afternoon she can get it now, but she's not going to be staying here tonight. I thought about it, but it's a better idea if Rachel stays over at the MGM. She can join Gillian and I at a couple of the after-parties, which I assumed you would probably not want to attend given your condition." Kelly shot a pointed glance at Marcy.

She smiled. "Thank you for thinking of that. You're right. I really don't want to attend any after-parties. If Rachel goes with you and Gillian, she'll be able to tell everyone that I was extremely tired and asked to be excused early. I'll mention feeling travel weary a couple of times during the evening and maybe even drop a hint or two about my condition. That'll take care of any speculation about where I'm staying."

"Excellent. Gillian and I are going to be leaving once you have finished with your cases, but before we go I want to touch base with Jeff and Mike." Kelly walked to a doorway on the far side of the sitting room and knocked twice.

The door opened immediately.

"You must be Kelly." An off-duty Las Vegas police officer stepped into the room and held his hand out. "I'm Jeff Moore, and this is my partner Mike Franklin."

Kelly shook Jeff's hand and then held his hand out to shake Mike's.

"I appreciate you guys being here. I'd like you to meet our client, Marcy Fischer and her sister Rachel Benson." Kelly introduced the two women who exchanged hellos with them. "And, this is my wife, Gillian."

Gillian stepped forward and shook hands with both of the men. "Thanks you very much for coming to my husband's aid. I know how relieved he was when your chief told Gus the two of you were willing to step in on your off time and help him out."

"I'd like to extend my thanks as well," Marcy spoke to the men. "I'm sure this is all a lot of worry about nothing, but I know I'm going to sleep a lot better at night because of all of you."

"Our pleasure, ma'am."

The two men returned to the other room and closed the door behind them.

Kelly turned back to Marcy. "They're going to be right next door the entire time. One of them will stay here even when we leave for the evening. What I want you to promise me is that you'll not leave this room without alerting them. I don't care if it's no further than the ice machine, please don't either you or Rachel leave the room without letting them know."

"I promise Kelly. After what happened in California, I'm not taking any chances at all. Whatever you say is what I'm going to do."

"Good. You and Rachel will have the rest of the afternoon and early evening for girl talk. If you want to order anything from room service, just knock on the door and give Jeff or Mike your order. They'll have your food delivered to their room and they'll bring it to you. Nobody in or out of this room until I return. The hotel has been instructed not to send anyone up to your room, maids or otherwise, and if anyone asks for admittance, you knock on the room next door and the boys will take care of them."

"Rachel and I will spend the entire day lounging around and recuperating from the past couple of days."

"I'll let you gals take care of those suitcases while I have a few words with Jeff and Mike. Gill, once you're ready just ring the bellman and have them come for the cases, then give me a yell next door. We'll meet the driver downstairs and head on over to the MGM."

They traveled by limousine to the MGM Grand where Kelly saw Gillian safely to the Skyloft, registered in Marcy's name.

He tipped the bellman and tucked the girls' luggage away in the adjoining room.

Gillian kicked her boots off and gazed at him intently. "We're finally alone."

Kelly scratched his chin. "As happy as I am about that, I've got to run a couple more errands before I can relax."

She started to protest but he placed a finger to her lips. "I won't be long." Removing his finger, he leaned down and planted a gentle kiss on her mouth. "I need you to remember that the staff thinks you're Marcy's personal assistant. Anyone who wants her will have to go through you. Got that?"

Nodding, she cupped the back of his head and pulled him close for one more kiss.

He chuckled. "Why don't you check out that giant Jacuzzi tub in the other room? Pour yourself something from the minibar, and relax. I'll be back before you know it."

She shot him a skeptical look. "You promise?"

Unable to resist, he pressed another kiss to her soft, sweet lips. "I absolutely promise. When I get back, I'll join you. I just need to confirm a few security details then I'll be able to relax and enjoy myself."

"This is supposed to be our honeymoon," she reminded.

He traced his thumb over her jawline. "That fact is not lost on me. I haven't forgotten in any way, shape or form. I'll do what I need to do, and be back in a flash."

"All right, then." She sauntered toward the large bathroom and cast a glance back over her shoulder. "After the week we've had, I feel like I'm about a hundred years old. Maybe some soaking and moisturizing'll keep me from looking like it, too."

He admired her shapely backside and shook his head. "No worries there, sugar. You just settle in. I'll see you soon." As he walked out, he switched on the sound system and the lyrics of a soft country ballad filled the room.

"Thank you!" she called.

"You betcha." He slipped out and closed the door behind him.

Kelly touched base with all the various entities who were assisting with security while they were in Vegas. Once he felt certain everyone knew his or her role, he leaned back in the limo and smiled. *Time to take care of some of the honeymoon stuff we're supposed to be enjoying on this trip.* "You know Sin City Cupcakes?" he asked the driver.

"Yes sir. It's maybe a ten minute drive."

"I'd like to go there, and if you could stop at a floral shop, I'd appreciate it."

Right on schedule, the driver pulled into the parking lot of the bakery. Kelly entered the shop and inhaled the delicious aroma. He studied the selections and chuckled at the names. When it was his turn to order, he smiled at the woman behind the counter. "Hi there. I'll have two Red Bull Cherry Bombs, two Better Than Sex — although I challenge that —" he grinned, "and two No Limit Lemon Drops."

"You won't be disappointed." She shot him a wink.

He nodded and paid as she handed over his boxed treats. He was certain she was right, but not so sure it would be because of the cupcakes.

A quick stop at a florist's shop so he could buy three dozen yellow roses, and he was on his way back to the hotel.

Armed with his gifts, Kelly entered the mirrored elevator and smiled at his reflection. It was finally starting to feel like a honeymoon.

He swiped his key card and opened the door to the suite. The first thing he spotted was Gillian, wrapped in a plush velour robe, curled up sound asleep on the sofa.

"Well, hell." He glanced at his watch. Even though he'd tried to hurry, he'd been gone nearly two hours. Of course she wouldn't still be in the Jacuzzi. She'd be a wrinkled prune if she was. He set the box of cupcakes down and found a makeshift vase for the flowers, then added water.

Kicking off his boots, he set them aside and unbuckled his belt.

Kelly leaned over the back of the sofa and pressed a light kiss to his wife's lips.

She stretched and yawned, her eyes still closed.

"Hey, Sleeping Beauty. Sorry I took so long. You want me to leave you alone?"

Gillian's eyes popped open. "Don't even joke about that. I was just resting for a few minutes. I'm awake." She ran the back of her hand over his cheek.

His heart melted, and he smiled at the beautiful expression on her face. "You are the most gorgeous creature I've ever laid eyes on. I love you more than words can say."

She chuckled. "I appreciate the sweet talk, but you do know I'm a sure thing, don't you?"

He grinned, and leaned in to nuzzle her neck. "I'd say the same thing even if you weren't. This wasn't intended to be a booty call. If you're tired and you'd rather just snuggle, I'm okay with that."

Gillian slid her arms around his neck. "You may be, but I'm not. I've been hanging out here fantasizing about you for the past two hours."

"Well then. I hope it included cupcakes and flowers." He nodded to the stand beside the couch where he'd placed his goodies.

"Oh my. Well they didn't up 'till now, but boy do I have some yummy ideas running through my mind." She reached out with one of her long fingers and swiped it across the top of a pink 'Hotter Than Sex'.

"Ooooh, woman, do you know what you've just done?"

She grinned. "Tell me."

"Why sugar, you've just scooped up a whole mouthful of 'Hotter Than Sex' and stuffed it in that hot little ol' mouth of yours."

Gillian couldn't help it. The way he rolled his eyes, the exaggerated Southern drawl, the hot pink cupcakes, all collided with her funny bone and she burst into hysterical laughter.

"Okay, woman, now back to what we were talking about before you got your fingers into icing sugar. Let's hear some more about this fantasizing you were doing while I was out tracking down treats for my sexy little bride. Come on, tell me more."

"Oh, I don't know. Just thinking about you, and what you're going to do to me."

"Mmm..." He rubbed his nose against hers. "What would you like me to do?"

She tightened her grip on his neck. "Nope, you're not making me do all the work. I got us this far. You take it from here."

He leaned back and reached for her hands. "Come on, then. Let's get this party started." He led her to their king-sized bed and released her hands long enough to toss the covers back.

Kelly faced Gillian and untied the belt on her robe, then pushed it off her shoulders. As he'd hoped, she was naked underneath. Her nipples pebbled when the air hit them, and his cock twitched at the delicious sight. "Damn. You're all nice and squeaky clean. I should probably hop in the shower real quick.”

“You do, and I’ll go out and find one of those off duty cops to finish what you started, buster.”

He laughed. “Oh yeah? Not in the mood to wait?”

“I’m in the mood, all right, but not to wait.” She batted her eyelashes at him. “You mentioned getting this party started?”

He stripped out of his clothes, kicking them out of his way. It felt amazing to be free of the tight jeans and boxers. His cock waved proudly the moment it was released.

Gillian licked her lips. “Now that’s more like it.” She reached for him.

Kelly stepped just out of her reach, then cupped her shoulders and pushed her backwards, gently, until she was prone on the bed. “Close your eyes.”

She set her jaw and gazed at him firmly. “Kelly McWinter, if you don’t join me in this bed right now—”

He pressed one finger to her lips. “Shhh. I intend to. Humor me first and close your eyes.”

Still appearing skeptical, she did as requested.

He hurried out to the table and grabbed one rose and one lemon cupcake. Returning to the bedroom, he set the cake on the nightstand and rubbed the fragrant rose across her cheek and under her nose.

She sniffed. “Mmm, nice.”

"Keep your eyes closed." He scooped a finger full of frosting and traced it across her lips.

Gillian tasted the sugary confection. "Oh my God, what is that heavenly flavor?"

He leaned down and kissed her, tasting for himself. He raised up enough to speak. "No Limit Lemon Drops. What kind of party would this be without cake?"

"More please." She smacked her lips.

Kelly chuckled. "Greedy girl." He broke off a bite of the cake and fed it to her. As she chewed, he turned the cupcake upside down and pressed the frosting against her nipple.

Gillian jumped, and a soft moan escaped her lips.

He grinned, twisting the cupcake against her other nipple. Before he set it down, he gave her one more bite.

"Mmm," she sighed.

Gazing at her frosting-covered breasts, he agreed. "Mmm hmm." Kelly licked one small mound until the sugar had melted and her rosy nubbin appeared. He sucked it into his mouth, his own desire growing as her nipple swelled.

She pressed her chest toward him, which was all the encouragement he needed. As he went to work cleaning her other breast, he rolled the first one between his thumb and forefinger.

"Oh God, Kelly. You're making me so hot." She squirmed beneath him, her gyrating becoming more intense the harder he teased her nipples.

He released the bud and blew on it. "You are hot. You're my hot wife."

She opened one eye just a crack. "About time for you to do something to cool me off, wouldn't you say?"

He reached between her legs and grinned at how wet she was. With his face mere inches from hers he whispered, "What do you want me to do, Gilly?"

Gillian bucked her hips. "You know what I want."

Kelly sucked a spot on her jawline, then pulled up again. "I do know. But I want to hear you say it. You told me that you like it when I talk dirty to you during sex. Well, I like it, too. So tell me, darlin', what do you want me to do to you?" His thumb found her clit and he rubbed little circles around it.

"Kelly!" she gasped, her hips darting up and down.

"I can quit, sugar. I'm sure there's a game on TV."

Her eyes widened and she glared at him. "You wouldn't dare!"

He laughed. "I wouldn't like it as much as I like this, but I might. Come on, Gilly. Talk dirty to me. Rev my engine up and let's see where we can go." He inserted two fingers into her tight channel as he continued to tease her clit.

"Aw, fuck!" she finally cried out. "Fuck me, darlin'! I need it bad. I need it now. Please, baby, I need to feel you inside me."

His heart soared and his cock throbbed. He needed it, too. Kelly raised Gill's hands over her head and held them there with one of his. With the other, he guided his aching erection deep inside her velvet-smooth opening. He gritted his teeth as he sank in deep. It wouldn't take much to set him off, but she was going to be good and satisfied before that ever happened.

Her first orgasm ripped through her within minutes. She hadn't needed to warn him, he felt it, and delighted in watching her eyes literally roll back in her head. He rocked her through that one then coaxed two more out before she'd had time to catch her breath.

They were both sweating profusely and he was sure neither of them cared. Kelly let go of her hands and clutched her hips, driving deeply a few more thrusts.

"I can't." She shook her head from side to side. "I'm spent."

"One more. Come with me, Gilly. I want to feel you pulsing around me. Your shudders will bring me home."

"Aw, God!" She grabbed his shoulders and looked him square in the eyes. "How can you do that to me? I swear, you could make me come with your voice if you wanted to."

Kelly grinned. "Good Lord willing, I'll never have to. Come on, baby. One more time. Bring it home." A few more strokes was all it took. Gillian shattered, her cries increasingly louder with each climax.

Her throaty wail sent him over the edge.

His orgasm struck swift and furious, and they were soon a tangled, panting mess of sweaty limbs. For a moment he wondered if he'd died and gone to heaven. When he could breathe again, and he studied the beautiful face of the women struggling to breathe beneath him, he knew he surely had.

Kelly's cell phone rang. *Texas When I Die.* He caught Gillian's eye and they gazed at each other for a moment.

She smiled. "At least Marcy has decent timing, I'll give her that."

He shook his head apologetically. "I don't want to answer it, but—"

"But it's your job and you have to. Go ahead. I'm a happy girl."

Grinning, he placed one more, quick kiss on her lips.

They both winced as he removed himself from their cozy position.

"Well, I *was* happy," she muttered jovially.

He grabbed his phone and pressed the talk button. "This is Kelly."

"Kelly, it's Marcy! You'll never believe what's happened!"

He scrubbed a hand over his face and moved the phone away. "Aw, fuck." Returning the cell to his ear he asked, "Are you okay?"

Chapter Seven

She's just as beautiful as I remembered her. The man fingered the 'Security' ID badge around his neck, proud that he'd been able to cover the photo on it so carefully with his own picture. No one had so much as batted an eyelash. He glanced down at the name on the badge. Thomas Keller. *Poor Mr. Keller, rotting in a storage closet in the basement.* He'd hidden the body so well, by the time it started to stink the ACM awards would be over and he'd be long gone—with Marcy Fischer by his side.

He ducked back inside Harrah's and hurried through the casino, losing himself in a section of penny machines. The cheap slots were busy all hours of the day, so it was an easy place to hide. Half the people playing there were sporting oxygen tanks and hearing aids. The rest were tourists down to their last few dollars, trying to make the money last longer by playing the cheaper slots. Their ignorance amused him. Gambling had never been his downfall.

Pausing by an elaborate Wizard of Oz machine with multiple chairs and players, he pretended to watch the game while keeping one eye on the door. No one seemed to be looking for him.

Marcy saw me. He'd never intended to get that close, but seeing her was almost like a drug for him. With that one glance it was as if he could smell her cherry blossom shampoo and the simple Dove soap she bathed with. Closing his eyes now, he recalled standing in her bathroom, inhaling the scent of the fragrances he'd found there. If only the stupid dog hadn't spotted him.

He shook his head. *No time for that now.* The past couldn't be changed, but the future was in his hands. The private investigator Marcy's stupid husband hired was hindering his plan, but not nearly as much as the cocky bastard thought he was. Mr. Kelly-Smart-Ass-McWinter had no idea that he'd already been in the presidential suite the PI had booked under his own name. *Amazing what doors the security badge open for me.* He'd listened to Kelly spell out the plan to Marcy and her sister, and to the two off-duty cops in the adjoining room.

Marcy had gone on and on about how complicated and organized it all sounded. *Little darling, you ain't seen nothing yet. I've been hatching my plan for months.* Not only for how he was going to get Marcy alone, but more importantly, for what he was going to do to her once they *were* alone.

He licked his lips. That was the best part. The ACM awards were playing nicely into his plans. The wing of hotel rooms undergoing a remodel would be deserted and secluded. Once he got Marcy there, he'd have all the time he needed. He licked his lips again.

* * *

Marcy's words came out in a rush. "Kelly, we went over to the Linc to do a bit of shopping, with both detectives in tow like I promised, and I spotted Lucas Spadina over there."

"Your crazy fan?"

"Yes."

"Are you sure it was him? There are lots of people in Vegas and it's easy to get confused with the crowds going by."

"It was him, Kelly. I'm sure of it."

He sighed, regretting their worst fears had been confirmed. "Okay. Where did you see him? What was he doing?"

"I saw him when we were walking through the passageway between Harrah's and the Linc. Rachel and I got bored sitting in the room, so I let the detectives know we wanted to do some shopping and they followed along behind us. We spent about an hour checking out the shops and getting a look at the High Rollers, then we headed back toward Harrah's."

"With both detectives following you?"

"Oh yes. They never at any time got very far behind us. They were very discreet, but they were keeping an eye on us the whole time."

"So very slowly tell me exactly what happened in regards to Spadina and how you know it was him."

"I don't know if you've walked between Harrah's and the Linc, but there's a kind of outdoor patio feel to it. They have buskers and food trucks, and a kind of pickup band, it's a cool spot and a lot of people pass through and take the time to check out entertainment. That's what Rachel and I were doing. The band was pretty good and we stopped to watch them when I spotted a guy come out from behind the stage they were using. He carried a tool box and had a cap pulled down to partially hide his face. When he got almost across from where we were standing, he looked up and I locked eyes with him. It was Lucas. No way I'm mistaken. He has the weirdest eyes, they're ice blue and sharp, like knife blades. I got a direct look at him when he tried to break into my place. I'd never seen eyes like that before and I'll never forget them. It was Lucas."

"Did you have my detectives make damn sure you weren't followed back to the room at Harrah's?"

"They sure did. I told them what I suspected and they took us all the way across to the Mirage, then piled us into a cab to take us back around through the shuttle and taxi entrances at Harrah's. They made us stay in the cab until they'd checked out the entire area. No one could possibly have followed us."

"Good. That's what I expected. I'm on my way over. We'll have to talk about this and decide how we want to proceed." Kelly punched the 'off' button on his phone and pocketed it.

He gave Gillian a quick kiss and left her snuggled down in the king sized bed with a satisfied smile on her face. "Damn I hate to leave. I'll be back as soon as I can."

She flashed him her sexiest grin and winked.

Kelly groaned as he let himself out the door. On the way down in the elevator he ordered the limo and his driver was there waiting when he reached the street.

If Marcy's right about Spadina being in town we've got to move quickly to convince him that the girls were just out shopping this afternoon and that the MGM Grand is their ultimate destination.

Kelly hopped into the front seat beside the driver and nodded a greeting. "Sorry for putting a rush on this, but it seems like our plans have to be moved up a bit. We're going to go over to Harrah's and pick up the ladies now. You'll drop us off at Caesar's Palace and we'll spend about forty-five minutes shopping. I'd like you to wait out front so when we're finished we'll all pile back in here and you can take us to the MGM Grand for the big entrance we talked about earlier."

The driver acknowledged the new instructions without any sign of frustration. Kelly sat back in the seat, going over the plan again, searching for loop holes. It seemed solid as far as he could tell.

He glanced at the driver. "How long until we get there?"

"Traffic is picking up. Fifteen minutes if we're lucky."

Kelly nodded. "Thanks." He pulled out his cell and hit the speed dial for Gus.

"Hey, boy, how are the bright lights and the big city?" his friend answered the call.

Kelly rubbed one temple. "A little too bright and big for my liking, old friend. Marcy says she saw her stalker this afternoon. I'm on my way to meet her and Rachel."

"Damn, I was hoping with you getting things all wrapped up in California you'd be partying it up tonight and heading home tomorrow."

"Sorry, looks like we might be looking at the second act right here in Vegas."

"You gotta do what you gotta do, but I'll be mighty glad to hear you've sets your boots back on home territory, if you know what I mean."

"It sounds like any thoughts I might have about taking a vacation from my honeymoon vacation are going to be out of the question."

"Hell Kelly, you know what it's like this time of year. Rodeo tryouts are in full swing, temperatures are heating up all over, and added to that the United Brotherhood and them damn Banditos are feuding again. I need you boy, real bad."

"I got you. Hopefully this will all be over with by tomorrow and once we get the girls home safe and sound, Gillian and I will be damn happy to head back to God's country."

"Good. I'm biding my time on this Azle business, but I need your input."

"I thought you were gonna call the Guard about those guys?"

"I did and as soon as I told them we were concerned about some guys out in the country with AK-47's they gave me the number of the ATF and told me to give them a call. I did that, and after I explained to them what we had to go on the sons-a-bitches politely told me to go sit on my thumb. Damn it all, Kelly, the only thing I had to give them was three missing teenagers, and what looked like a private military training field. They perked up at that one, but when I told them you hadn't been able to identify any particular organization, they told me they'd see if they had anyone available and let me know if it warranted their attention. In other words, 'go sit on a tack'."

"Piss you off did they?"

"Assholes. But truth is we've got no grounds to bring anybody in for questioning. What I need is someone to do some more nosing around."

"I see what you mean. You know I've been thinking about what direction I wanted to go with the PI firm, what with Gillian's stables growing the way they are and my private work doing the same. I think maybe we need to sit down and have a talk when I get back."

"Sounds damn good to me, just as long as you don't come up with any confaluting idea about hanging up your shield. Hell, it was pulling teeth to get you on as a contractor and now that the higher ups know how good you are, they want me using you on every job."

"I gotcha. That's what we need to talk about. Maybe I need to clone myself."

"You do that. I'll take as many of you as they make. As long as they're licensed and have the creds, we'll be good to go.

"You can be a pain in my ass, you know that, Gus?"

"Right back atcha, you lucky sum'bitch. I gotta go for now. We're getting a real toad choker of a rainstorm. That bridge over Indian Creek will be impassable soon and I'm fixin' to see they get the warning signs up."

"We can use the moisture, I guess."

"Not all in one God damn night."

"Good luck with that."

"Talk to you later Kelly."

"Yep." He ended the call, and tried not to let uneasiness about things in Texas crowd his thoughts. Marcy came first, and he was determined to focus on her until the awards show was over and he could put her and Rachel back on a plane. At that point, he'd have one more honeymoon night with Gillian, and he was hoping to make it a special one. Blake Shelton had agreed to meet up with them for drinks at the *Warner Music Nashville After-Party*, since he was now in Vegas for the awards. Kelly hadn't told his wife, in case the plans fell through again. If it worked out, she'd be tickled as hell.

He smiled. *When mama's happy, everyone's happy.*

* * *

Kelly rode the elevator up to the presidential suite and escorted Marcy and Rachel back down to the limo. As directed, the driver left them off at Caesar's Palace so the sisters could shop. Kelly followed along behind, carrying bags and keeping a sharp eye out. To his relief the trip was uneventful and there were no more Spadina sightings.

Gillian met them in the lobby of the MGM with a couple of bellhops to carry their purchases. The additional men made their group larger, and thanks to Gillian's efforts, noisier, thereby attracting more attention. When they were finally alone in the Skyloft, Kelly dropped into a chair.

Gillian sat on the armrest next to him. "Good Lord. I'm not sure we could have made a bigger scene."

He smiled. "That's what we were after. People now know where Marcy is staying, and she'll be seen leaving to go to the awards."

Marcy rubbed her upper arms nervously. "I'm concerned about y'all staying here now, when all the security is over at Harrah's with me."

"I've got a guy here to keep an eye on Rachel's room. Not taking any chances with the kid after LA. Gill and I will be fine."

His wife rubbed the back of his neck lightly.

He glanced up and caught her smile.

"Yes, we will," she agreed, then turned her gaze to Marcy. "Do you want to rest a while before you need to get ready?"

"Maybe." Marcy nodded and stood.

Gillian rose with her. "Come on. You can lie down in the room at the end of the suite."

"Thanks. I need to call Mark, too. He wants to wish me luck before we go."

"I just know you're going to win!" Rachel enthused.

Marcy waved a hand as she headed down the short hall. "Stop. I'm just happy to be nominated." She and Gillian disappeared as they entered the back bedroom.

Kelly grinned at Rachel. "They all say that."

Rachel jumped up and struck a dramatic pose, speaking into a pretend microphone. "It's an honor just to be nominated! What a bunch of BS!"

He laughed and watched Rachel flop back onto the sofa. "It is, you know. Not everyone can win. Your sister should be proud of all she's accomplished this year."

"The nominees all have those frozen smiles on their faces because they know the cameras are everywhere. Then, when someone else's name is called, they have to clap politely and look happy for a winner *that's not them.*"

"It's all part of it, I guess. Think how many new singers enter the scene each year. Only five get singled out. Like I said, she can be damn proud."

Rachel stood and waved her hand flippantly. "She's going to win, so it doesn't matter. I just feel it in my bones."

He smiled. "I hope you're right."

The girl grinned. "I just know I am! I want to start doing my hair." She ran into Gillian in the hall. "Where will I find my things?"

"Right back here. We figured you two would like to get ready together." She pointed Rachel to another bedroom in the suite.

"Great. Thanks!" Rachel slipped into the room and closed the door.

Gillian returned to her seat next to Kelly. "She's *so* excited. More than Marcy, I believe."

He lifted her hand and caressed it. "I think you're right. I just hope she won't be too disappointed if Marcy doesn't win."

Gillian frowned. "You don't sound too sure about her chances."

Kelly shrugged. "One in five. Four talented ladies will have to go home remembering that it *is* an honor to be nominated, despite how lame that sounds."

She leaned in and pressed a kiss on his forehead. "You're right. I just hope that's our only worry this evening."

He slid an arm around her waist. "You and me both, babe."

Within the next hour, Kelly watched with amusement as the frenzy to look perfect for the evening kicked into high gear. He was used to one woman monopolizing his space but three was more than he'd bargained for. First chance he got, he took his tuxedo and a few things to the smallest bathroom, giving the ladies free reign of the rest of the suite.

The Academy of Country Music awards were held in the Garden Arena at the MGM. Entertainers used a special secure entrance, and once Kelly had gotten his group that far he relaxed considerably. Security in the Arena was out in full force. He glanced around, satisfied that everything seemed under control.

He slid an arm around Gillian's waist and pressed a kiss to her temple.

She smiled and whispered in a hushed voice, "There's more bodyguards in here than there are Tony Lama boots, I'd wager."

Grinning, he spoke into her ear. "Which is just the way I like it. The more protection the better."

She gazed around the Arena. "Our little Marcy isn't the biggest fish in the pond. There's Miranda Lambert. Lordy, look at her entourage!"

Rachel leaned in. "When Marcy gets that big, are you going to head her security detail Kelly?"

He shook his head. "I don't think so, sugar. There are people specially trained for that line of work. I just do it in a pinch."

Gillian squeezed his arm. "I'd trust you before I'd trust any ten of those guys."

He chuckled. "You wouldn't be a smidge prejudiced now would you? And by the way, in case I haven't told you in the last ten minutes, you look gorgeous tonight."

She reached up and kissed his cheek. "You've told me about fifty times, but I never get tired of hearing it." Rising on her toes to whisper in his ear, Gillian added, "And the only thing sexier than you in that monkey suit will be you, *out of the monkey suit*, later tonight."

His hand slid down and patted her butt. "Right back at'cha, babe." Kelly kissed his wife once more, then they were at the front of the line and ready to be seated in the VIP section. "Here we go."

They all exchanged glances and smiles.

* * *

Inside the room adjoining Marcy's suite the two detectives had settled into chairs and were watching the images of a road race on the television screen.

"Not quite the same without the roar of the engines," Mike remarked.

"Yeah," Jeff agreed, "but we need to keep our ears tuned to anything out of order next door. At least we get to watch some action. Beats sitting out in a car spying on somebody's wife."

"There's that," Mike laughed. "Personally I don't know how the PI's do it; not that I don't appreciate the extra income that comes from moonlighting, but gigs like this are a lot more my style than what the agencies normally have to offer."

"Kelly's a good guy. I—" A noise outside their door got his attention. "Hello, what's that?" Jeff stood and walked over to the door and glanced out the peephole before pulling it open. "Can I help you?" He spoke to the security guard holding a tray with a coffee canister and two cups.

"Kitchen asked me to drop this off to you fellas." The skinny guard with large glasses and slightly longish hair, dipped his head and smiled tentatively. "Do you want me to put it on the table?"

"No, that's okay, I'll take it. Nice of them to remember. Thanks." Jeff reached in his pocket for a dollar bill and handed it over.

"Have a nice evening." The guard pocketed the money and turned away.

"That's damn good timing." Mike said from his seat at the table. "My eyes were starting to get heavy."

"Yeah, mine too." Jeff set the tray on the table and poured out two cups of the steaming black liquid. "Kelly must have asked them to send some up. Like I said, he's a good guy."

They settled back with their cups and returned to watching the silent race.

* * *

They'll be sleeping like babies in no time. Lucas chuckled to himself as he headed down the hall, then ducked into one of the rooms in the section of the hotel that was in the process of being renovated. *I'll give them ten minutes, that should be plenty of time.* He checked his watch a couple of times and then, when enough time had passed, he picked up another canister of coffee and set off down the hall,

138

back to the room where the two detectives were.

Lucas listened at the door a minute before using his master key card to enter. He had a gun *and* a knife, in the event one of them had decided not to drink the spiked coffee. Lucky for them, they were both passed out in their chairs, sprawled with legs spread out and their chins balanced on their collar bones.

Howdy fellas. Hope you're enjoying your little snooze. Lucas snickered at the two men. *Let's just take that pot outta here, so no one gets any bright ideas about it being laced with knockout drops.* He picked up the tray with the pot and two cups and took them into the bathroom. After he washed out the two cups, he returned the tray with both cups to the table. Taking the old pot and setting it aside, he poured half a cup of coffee into each cup from the new pot he'd brought with him, and then took the drugged pot with him out the door. Stopping in front of the suite next to the room he'd just left, he used his master key, opened the door of the suite and let himself inside.

Well now, that went just like I expected. He congratulated himself as he walked around the suite where his beloved Marcy would soon be coming to spend the night. *It's going to be just you and I tonight, my darling.* He smiled and clapped his hands like a small child anticipating a special treat. *Oh yes. Tonight all my hopes and dreams are going to come true and you're truly going to be mine forever.*

As he pranced around the room with the coffee canister in his arms, he opened the door to a closet and moved aside the extra pillows kept there for the convenience of guests. Placing the canister on the shelf, he replaced the pillows and blanket so that the canister was pushed to the back and not visible to anyone opening the closet.

"Best get myself settled. Those two next door should be waking up anytime and we don't want them hearing any noises and coming in to investigate, now do we?" He continued talking to himself as he strolled through the suite, searching for the best hiding place.

"Well now, what have we here?" He stopped in front of a large chest with a padded seat. Lifting the lid, he removed the large quilt that had been stored inside and carried it over to the closet with the pillows. The quilt was too large to fit on the shelf, but not expecting anyone to look inside the closet anyhow, with the bed already crowded with more pillows than any one person would be likely to use, he set it on the floor and closed the door.

He yanked the trunk away from the wall to examine it. *Might be a bit snug but I won't mind that.* There was the matter of getting enough air. Pulling out his knife, he stabbed holes in the particleboard backing of the trunk, where no one could see them. Smiling to himself, he re-pocketed the knife and shoved the heavy piece back into place before he climbed inside.

Now all I need to do is lay back and pretend I'm snuggled in with my love bug. That'll keep me nice and cozy. A high pitched laugh squeaked out before he cut himself off, mindful of the two detectives who'd likely be waking soon. Climbing inside, he pulled his legs up until they rested against his backside and squeezed his arms together so that with a nudge of his head the lid dropped into place. *Snug as a bug.* Smiling, he closed his eyes and settled down to wait.

Chapter Eight

Jeff opened his eyes and shook his head. *Son of a bitch. Did I let myself drop off to sleep?* He cursed and looked over at Mike.

What the hell? Both of us sleeping? He reached over and shook Mike's shoulder.

"Hey, what's up?" Mike jerked awake and look around, shaking himself like a big dog. "Sorry man, I must have fallen asleep."

Jeff cleared his throat and replied with a gruffness he didn't feel on the inside. "Don't let it happen again." His mind raced. *Can't have been too long, the race is still going.* Jeff glanced at the speeding cars flashing by on the screen. He walked over and placed his ear to the door of the adjoining suite. "There's no sound coming from in there." He rejoined Mike at the table. "How about we play a few hands of cribbage?" Jeff got a board and a deck of cards out of his briefcase and set them up on the table.

"Uh, sure." Mike took their coffee cups over to the sink, poured out the cold coffee and returned to the table where he opened the canister and poured them two fresh cups of the still-hot liquid.

Jeff nodded. *This'll keep us awake and we can shut that television off. Watching those cars spin round and round the track is probably what lulled us to sleep in the first place.*

"Good idea." Mike picked up the remote and clicked the off button. "I don't care as much about it without the sounds of the engines racing anyhow."

Jeff reached for the deck and lifted up a small stack of cards. "Cut for deal."

* * *

After the awards show ended and Marcy had delivered her 'It was an honor to be nominated' line to every reporter in sight, Kelly ushered them all out the doors and back to the limo.

"Sorry, Sis." Rachel squeezed Marcy's hand.

"It's fine, really. The show was amazing and it was such an incredible experience. I'm so happy you all could be there with me."

"It was pretty awesome," Gillian agreed. "You look beat. Good thing Kelly's riding back to Harrah's with you."

"There's really no need." Marcy waved a hand. "The minute I get back I'm going straight upstairs, to peel out of these clothes and scrub my face."

"That's exactly what we're expecting you to do," Kelly agreed. "Meantime, I'll just ride along, take a quick look inside the suite before I lock you in for the night." He put his hand under Marcy's elbow to assist her into the back seat of the limo.

"I'll be back in about an hour," he told Gillian. "We've got an invite to the *Warner Music Nashville After Party*. You'll see more stars inside that room than in these skies where Mother Nature's damn near swallowed up by manmade luminaries."

Rachel's eyes sparkled. "That sounds so fun."

Kelly nodded. "I'll go get Marcy situated and touch base with Jeff and Mike and then I'll be back to join you. Stay out of trouble." He winked at Gillian and bent down to give her a quick kiss before circling around the limo and climbing in the front seat beside the driver.

Gillian opened the door on Marcy's side, while Kelly was walking around and whispered to the exhausted-looking singer. "I had some room service delivered. I requested several flavors of ice cream. I figured, you know..." She shrugged. "Win or lose, ice cream never hurts."

Marcy smiled. "Thanks Gill. That sounds perfect. As soon as Kelly checks the room, I'll fix myself a huge bowl then crawl into bed and call Mark, so he can gush over me and soothe any wounds that might be open a little."

"Great See you tomorrow." Gillian closed the door and stepped back to the sidewalk with Rachel. "Shall we go inside and see who's with who and how the stars act when the spotlights are turned off?" She linked her arm with Rachel's and the two of them headed back inside the MGM.

* * *

Kelly glanced in each room of Marcy's suite before rejoining her in the sitting area. "Rocky Road, huh?" He nodded toward the container of ice cream she'd chosen.

She smiled back and shrugged sheepishly. "Yeah, well, it *is* an honor to be nominated. But Gillian was right, ice cream never hurts."

He grinned. "You take it easy. I'm going to touch base with the guys next door before I leave."

"Have a nice night, Kelly. Thanks again for everything."

"You bet, sugar." He nodded and pulled her door closed behind him. He rapped on the next door and waited.

Jeff Moore pulled the door open. "Hey, Kelly. How were the awards? Did Marcy win?"

He stepped into the room. "Nope, but she took it like a trooper. All the girls were excited to be there and see the stars. My wife is back there now, anxiously awaiting my return. There's an after party that Blake Shelton is supposed to attend. I'll be a dead

145

duck if I don't get her there to at least say hi."

Mike Franklin spoke up. "Go ahead and have fun. We've got things under control here. The coffee you sent up hit the spot by the way, thanks."

Something about Marcy's room was niggling at the back of Kelly's mind, but he couldn't put his finger on exactly what. He nodded at Mike absently. "Okay, well here's to a quiet night. You've got my number if you need it. Don't hesitate to call. Of course if it's serious, call nine-one-one first. Let's not take any chances."

Jeff waved a hand. "We got this. No worries. Have a nice night, and we'll see you in the morning."

"Yeah. Thanks." Kelly backed out and pulled the door closed. The men had been referred by a friend of Gus' so he felt sure they were competent, but they didn't seem to be taking the job that seriously. He shrugged his shoulders to work out the kinks as he rode the elevator down. *Maybe I'm overthinking things.* As Gillian had commented, Marcy wasn't the biggest fish in the pond. A bunch of fanatics weren't after her. It was just the *one* that concerned him.

Lucas Spadina had been spotted in the city, and like Gus, Kelly didn't believe in coincidence. The small hairs on the back of his neck prickled as he stepped out into the lobby. *They keep these casinos ice cold.* As he walked out, he tried to convince himself that was the reason for his goosebumps. Deep down, he knew it wasn't.

A pall of general uneasiness settled over him, but he pasted on a smile and tried to be pleasant as he escorted Gillian and Rachel to the after party. Blake Shelton's gentlemanly charms didn't disappoint, and Gillian was *almost* as happy as if they'd had dinner with the superstar. A few hours later by the time they'd mingled until his cheeks were tired of smiling, he dropped Rachel off in her room and escorted his wife to theirs.

Gillian tugged at his bowtie. "You're worse than my stallion waiting for his mares to arrive." She patted his chest and offered her lips for a quick kiss. "I understand. You're worried about Marcy. You won't fully relax until this job's over with and you've delivered her safely home to Nashville."

Kelly grinned and pulled her into his arms. "I'm sorry, love. There's no reason I can't settle down and enjoy the hell out of what's supposed to be our honeymoon, but something keeps niggling at my mind."

"Like what? Did you see something off over there, or was it some*one* that didn't fit?"

"Nope. Nothing like that. The guys were all settled in next door. Marcy's got the buzzer if anything happens, and everyone seemed settled. She was eating Rocky Road ice cream, and said to tell you that you're a woman after her own heart."

"I thought it might help. I know she's not devastated by the loss, and she is genuinely happy for Miranda, but she wouldn't be human if there wasn't a bit of residual hurt."

He pressed another kiss to his wife's forehead. "You're right, as usual. How'd I get so lucky to marry you?"

Gillian rose up on her toes and gazed into his eyes. "Funny, I thought *I* was the lucky one." She kissed him and melted into his arms.

Kelly embraced her and maintained the kiss as he walked her backwards to the settee. His fingers found her zipper and lowered it, at the same time he settled her onto her back.

She nimbly unbuttoned his shirt then used both hands to push it and his jacket from his shoulders.

His tongue batted against hers for a few more minutes before he couldn't resist any longer, and allowed his mouth to wander. Over to one earlobe, where he licked around her pearl earring.

She moaned then gasped as his lips moved lower, kissing a warm trail down the column of her neck.

"Damn, Kelly," she murmured, her voice breathy.

"Mmm hmm," he agreed, but didn't stop. At the base of her neck, he sucked noisily, marking her fair skin with a purple love bite.

"Hey!" She twitched. "That smarts."

Nuzzling her collarbone, he smiled. "You want me to stop?"

Gillian's reply came out with a rush of air. "God, no!"

He grinned and continued south, dragging her dress and strapless bra down together. Her rosy nipples peaked when cool air hit them, and it was Kelly's turn to groan. "Damn, woman. Just the sight of you makes me hard."

She ran her hands through his hair and mussed it. "What are you gonna do about it? Or should I say, prove it."

Capturing one nubbin between his teeth, he murmured, "Soon enough. I've got more tasting to do. *Lots more.* Mmm, and this is so much better than ice cream."

She chuckled. "If you say so. But if we're going to be here long, we might need to pull this settee out. My head's buttin' the wall, sugar."

He buried his face between her breasts. "I never was very good at pulling out."

Gillian laughed out loud. "God, you're incorrigible. I surely do love you. But I'd really like you to stop for two minutes and move this thing away from the wall."

Kelly's heart caught in his throat. "Oh, shit!" He bolted upright.

She smiled at him. "It's not that big of a problem, just a little uncomfortable."

"I remember what's been bothering me!" He stood and paced. "There was a big trunk in Marcy's suite. I barely gave it a glance, but now I recall that it'd been moved since this afternoon. I could tell by the marks on the floor."

She sat. "Who would move it? The cleaning people had already been in."

He reached for his shirt. "I left strict instructions for no one to enter her room." Shirt in hand, he looked at his wife apologetically.

She lifted her dress and covered her breasts. "Go on. We won't have a moment's peace until you've checked on her again. In fact, maybe you should just sleep on her sofa."

Kelly raced to button his shirt and retrieve his guns from the counter where he'd left them. "I shouldn't need to do that."

Gillian stood. "Baby, do what you came here to do. We've got the rest of our lives together. This..." she pointed to them and the settee, "as nice as it is, can wait. Go on, now. I love you. Grab some coffee on your way. It might be a long night."

As he holstered his gun Kelly's heart sank remembering Mike Franklin's words. *The coffee you sent up hit the spot.* He'd been intent on hurrying back to Gillian. *He* was the one who hadn't taken things seriously enough. "I didn't send up any god-damned coffee!" He hurried to the door.

"What?" Gillian blinked, confused.

He shook his head. "Call Marcy, *now*. Make sure she's okay. I'll call Franklin and Moore on my way down, after I've phoned my driver."

Gill bit her lip. "All right."

Kicking himself six ways from Sunday, Kelly nodded gravely and slipped out the door.

* * *

Marcy stuck the ice cream container back into the freezer then went to brush her teeth and wash her face. She'd eaten enough to make herself sick during the thirty minute phone conversation with Mark. They normally didn't talk that long, but he was homesick and felt bad for missing the awards. Marcy assured him it'd been a good show to miss. Hopefully, she had a long career ahead of her, and there'd be other awards. Maybe even a win.

Her cosmetics were spread out on the counter and she paused, knowing she hadn't left them that way. Had Rachel gone through her things earlier? It seemed unlikely, considering they'd dressed at Harrah's.

A chill ran up her spine and Marcy glanced up at the dressing room mirror.

"Hello, beauty." Lucas Spadina's icy blue eyes stared back at her reflection.

She jumped, grabbing the counter for support.

151

He chuckled. "Take it easy, there. I'm excited, too, but there's no need to jump out of your skin."

Marcy blinked. "My husband is on his way. He'll be here any minute."

Lucas smiled. "Is that so? Does he have a teleportation device? Because I just heard your drearily long-winded conversation with him, and the best I can tell he's still in Russia. Else he would have been at the awards tonight, correct?"

Her mind raced. "Okay, you're right. But you know he provided me with a bodyguard, right? Kelly just went to get a bite to eat. He'll be—"

Lucas took a step closer. "He'll be here any minute, I know. The problem with that is, I heard him say he was going back to Harrah's to be with his little wifey. The other problem is that you've now lied to me twice, my love. Ever heard of the three strike rule?"

Holding as still as a statue, Marcy watched him in the mirror.

"Speak to me when I ask you a question, please."

The eerie calmness in his voice frightened her more than his steely gaze. "I'm sorry I lied," she said slowly.

He shook his head sadly. "I don't sense true conviction in that answer. I'd envisioned this evening going a whole different way, but you've made me unhappy and now I just want to get this over with."

Fear coursed through her veins. "I'm sorry! What can I do to make you happy?" Marcy gasped at her own words. A couple of things came to her sane, rational mind. She couldn't bear to imagine what his sick, twisted brain might be thinking.

Lucas laughed. "Now you're talking. Making me happy should be your number one priority. And just so you know, *keeping* me happy means keeping you alive."

She closed her eyes. *This isn't going to end well.*

Her phone and the panic button were both next to the bed. Perhaps, if he took her there, she could make a grab for them. But the bed was the last place she wanted to be with Spadina. "Wha—what do you want?"

He brandished a hunting knife and traced it lightly across her shoulder. "What do I want? Good question. I'd originally planned to take you to an empty wing of the hotel where we could have some privacy, but your bumbling security guards don't scare me all that much. I think we'll just stay here. As long as you're quiet, we won't have a problem, now, will we?" He pressed the point of the knife against her neck.

A single tear ran down her cheek. Marcy blinked, trying to remain strong. "I'll be quiet. Just please, don't hurt me."

"Hurt you?" he scoffed. "I never would have considered hurting you, until I heard bits and pieces of conversation that I found troubling. I'm going to ask you another question, Marcy my love, and I promise you one thing. If you lie to me again, I'll slice you wide open." He moved the knife to her stomach.

Marcy gasped and tried to shirk away. "I won't lie!" she sobbed.

"Are you pregnant?"

She hesitated. That was the last thing she wanted him to know, but lying was no longer an option. "Yes."

He frowned and shook his head. "Now you see, that just disturbs me. I'd envisioned you and I going away together, but I'd never factored a kid into the picture. I just don't think that's going to work out."

Her hands went instinctively to protect her belly. "I'm sorry. If you want to leave, please, just go. I won't tell anyone you were here. You could sneak out and no one will ever know. I promise."

"Given our recent track record, I'm not sure I can believe you, sweetheart. You've lied to me twice already."

Tears were streaming, now, and Marcy was unable to control them. "No more lies!" She shook her head.

He leaned in from behind and pressed his face to her neck, inhaling deeply. "You smell so sweet, like cherry blossoms and something else. What is that delicious aroma?" He caught her gaze in the mirror. Eyes wide, she appeared terrified.

Just the way I want her. He licked her neck and chuckled as she shrank away.

"Delightful. Let's go to the bedroom and get comfortable." With his knife blade at her waist, he led her to the hall. "Which bedroom are you in?"

She pointed to the left.

Lucas pushed her forward, into the room on the right.

Marcy tried to protest but he reminded her of the knife and she cooperated.

He chuckled. "Oh yes, I remember the other fragrance. Fear. I just love the scent of fear."

She opened her mouth to scream but he covered it with his hand, and kicked the door closed behind them.

* * *

Kelly raced down the hall to Marcy's room. Franklin and Moore were standing outside, rattling the door.

He pulled his gun. "Why aren't you in there?"

"The passkey won't open it. The hotel is sending someone up."

Kelly glanced from side to side. "And where the hell are the police?"

"We called them," Franklin insisted. "It's a busy night, and we didn't have much to go on."

Fuming with anger, Kelly shook his head. "You mean to tell me hotel security couldn't get here any faster, either?"

Franklin shrugged and shook his head.

Shaking the door once more, Kelly made a decision. He was in no mood to wait. "Fuck this." He took aim at the knob and fired.

The sound resonated in the hall and both of the cops jumped at the noise. The shot had the desired effect as the frame crumbled and the door popped open. He glanced at them. "Back me up."

"You got it." They drew their guns and followed him into the suite.

Weapon at the ready, Kelly assessed the front room quickly and continued down the hall. The sound of gunfire had pretty much taken away the element of surprise. "Marcy!" he yelled.

"Mmm!" Muffled hollering echoed from the back bedroom.

His back to the wall, he inched around the corner and spotted her, nightclothes shredded, gagged with her hands tied to the headboard. "Where is he?" Kelly mouthed.

She nodded toward the other door.

He went to her side, tossing a sheet over her as he removed her gag. "Where'd he go?"

"He took off when the gun went off. That way." She nodded again.

Kelly was torn, desperately wanting to pursue but hating to leave her. "Are you okay?"

Marcy nodded quickly. "He didn't have time to do anything."

"Thank God. I hate to leave you but—"

"I'm okay. Go! Be careful! He's crazy as a bedbug, Kelly."

He turned to Franklin. "Stay with her." Pointing to Moore he added, "Come on." They took off out the back way, shooting off another lock in lieu of a passkey. They ran down several flights of stairs but Kelly knew at that point it was useless. Spadina could have stopped and gotten lost on any floor.

He slapped the metal door in front of him angrily. "Fuck!"

Moore holstered his gun. "Let's call it in. We've got a description, the police will be all over it now."

"Well that's just fucking fine." Kelly stomped back up the way they'd come, and found the bedroom full of hotel security and police.

A large man with a crew cut and stocky build confronted him. His nametag indicated he was MGM security. "Who the hell gave you permission to fire your weapon in the building?"

Kelly could have decked him. "If your team would have gotten up here faster, I might not have needed to."

"This is a big hotel, sir."

"It sure as shit is. And you've got a lunatic running around in it as we speak. So you can stand here and give me grief, or you can get as many people as possible on the lookout for Lucas Spadina. He's most like armed."

"He has a knife," Marcy added.

Franklin had untied her hands and she was sitting on the bed, the sheet wrapped around her.

Kelly sighed. "Are you sure you're okay?"

She nodded. "It's a damn good thing you got here when you did, though. I'm not foolin', he's batshit crazy, Kelly."

He sat next to her and put one arm around her shoulder. As he suspected, she was shaking. He could tell by her language that she wasn't holding up as well as she was trying to let on. Pulling out his phone, he dialed Gillian.

"Oh thank God!" his wife answered with a rush of air. "I haven't been able to reach Marcy and Rachel and I are worried sick."

"She's okay, but Spadina was here. Listen to me, this is what I want you to do. Call your driver, ask him to pick you up in thirty minutes. I'm going to phone the hotel and have security escort you and Rachel to the limo. Tell the driver you're going to—" He glanced up at the nearest police officer. "What hospital?"

"Sunrise on Maryland Parkway."

Kelly repeated into the phone, "Sunrise Hospital on Maryland Parkway. I'll meet you at the emergency entrance."

Gillian gasped. "I thought you said Marcy was okay? Are you hurt?"

"I'm pissed, but I'm not hurt. We need to have her checked out. Once she's been cleared, we're packing our shit and getting the hell out of here. I don't care what time it is, we're going to Nashville tonight."

Chapter Nine

Gus looked up from his desk at the tall, dark-haired young man who'd tapped on his office door before stepping in. Sunglasses hanging from one pocket, his thick head of hair appeared wind-blown and disheveled. The kid had obviously needed a shave three days ago. His wrinkled, button-down work shirt fell untucked over jeans, and Gus saw a hint of a badge poking out from under the tail. *This can't be good.* "Can I help you?"

"I hope so. I'm Cade Wyatt, Special Agent with the ATF. Sent over here by the Deputy Director to check out the situation you might have brewing."

Gus cocked his head and squinted at him. "I thought you guys were too damn important to waste time on a bunch of yahoos out in Azle?"

The kid gave a belly laugh. "That'd be the other guys. Me, I'm mostly what they call a pain in the ass. They probably sent me over here to get me out of the way and make you feel like those boys could hardly wait to solve y'all's little problem out there."

"Damned if you don't remind me of someone else I know." Gus shook his head.

"Did they brief you on what we suspect might be going on out there?"

"Sort of. I wouldn't mind hearing it from you, though."

Gus folded his hands on his desk. "Initially we thought we had a probationer gone missing. Wade Clements got himself arrested for hacking into a DOD computer. Kid wasn't too malicious about it and the judge gave him ninety days probation. Seems Clements' older brother was killed in action over in Afghanistan, and the judge cut the kid some slack. And, as per usual, no god-damned good deed goes unpunished. Clements skipped out and we're left trying to track him down."

Cade leaned forward. "You have a recent picture of him?"

Gus shuffled some papers on his desk and came up with the most recent mugshot. He shoved it to the other side of his deck.

The agent picked it up and studied it. "He'd be about twenty-two now?"

"Sounds right." Gus rubbed his chin. "Add to that, we've got three missing teenage boys who, coincidentally, have also lost fathers or brothers in the service."

Cade studied the picture another moment before making eye contact with Gus. "I don't know about you, but I don't believe in coincidence."

Gus smiled. "I suspected you might feel that way. Most of the people I trust do. I have a PI that I use for this type of stuff, a good man. Kelly McWinter. He nosed around out in Azle where the Clements' family supposedly owns some land and came upon what looked like a military training operation. Fellas with AK-47's."

"Aw shit. What'd he do?"

"He got the hell outta there, that's what he did. He was in no position to confront them. He suggested we call in the guard, but they referred me to the ATF. Which is apparently where you come in."

With a small wave of his hand, Cade nodded. "Guilty as charged. I can tell you, we've been aware of various WAM branches popping up regionally. Western American Militia. Have you heard of them?"

Nodding, Gus frowned. "Bunch of nutcases. Kelly calls them 'home-grown crazies'."

"That's accurate. Sounds like we might have a chapter forming here."

"Well now, I'd be happy as hell to shut that thing down before it gets any bigger."

Cade grinned. "And I'd be happy as hell to help you. So what can you tell me about this place they're camped at?"

"Some, but not much. I pulled the latest plat on file for that property." Reaching for a rolled sheaf of paper, he spread it out across his already cluttered desk. "Here's the line shack Kelly saw. There's not much else on the grounds for a few miles. But if you follow this dirt road back a ways, you find this." Gus's finger hit a big square indicating a building of significant size. "The main ranch house."

Cade stood and leaned over the desk to study the plat. "Have you gotten a satellite image?"

"Yep." Gus shuffled through the stack for another image. "This here's a print out of the photo, shows what we can see of the property. Here's that line shack and right there's the road that leads everywhere *except* back to the house. But check this out." He pointed to a large flat area, nestled between rolling hills.

"Holy shit." Cade stared down at a line of military Humvees and network of barb-wired trenches. Twenty or thirty men were photographed in the slightly distorted image. "It looks like a training field at Fort Hood!"

"Yes indeed. And it seems like they've erected a lot of new bunkhouses and sheds back of the main house that don't show up on that plat."

The agent studied the photo for a minute. "So if the road doesn't run past the house, how do they get in and out?"

Gus glanced at him. "All roads lead through the training area. I'm guessing a four-wheel drive vehicle could take you to the house. They prolly drive Jeeps and trucks."

Cade smiled. "I drive a Jeep."

"Don't get any bright ideas. We don't have probable cause to go out there in connection with any case we're working on, and we don't have grounds for a search warrant."

He smiled innocently. "What? We'd just be canvassing the area and talking to some folks. All we're doing is looking for some missing kids. That's well within our duties and we're not goin' to be conducting any property searches. I just want to see what's what, that's all. Get a better feeling about the place."

Gus placed his palms on his desk. "I agree you need to see the place, but we're not near ready to talk to anyone. We'll go out there and nose around. If it looks promising, maybe you report back to the ATF and they can send you some backup."

"The ATF ain't interested in three teenage boys who've gone AWOL on their mamas. I'll be honest with you, they don't think your lead's going to turn out to be worth much. It makes them look good if they send an agent, and like I said they liked the idea of getting me outta their hair and into yours."

Gus nodded. "So what are you thinking?"

"I'm gonna need to get in there. They'll want real proof that something bigger is going on. If we can get that, they'll send backup. Until then, I'm confident I can handle it."

Gus liked this kid. Reminded him of Kelly in the early days. Cocksure and raring to go crazy. *Best keep an eye on him.* He nodded grudgingly. "Seein' as to how you can't make much of an assessment without surveying the scene, I'll take you out there. But no crazy stuff. I'm still a good shot, but I ain't quite as spry as I used to be, should we need to manage a quick getaway."

Cade smiled. "You won't need to be."

"All right, then. Why don't you drop into the break room across the hall while I finish up one report." Gus waved his arm across the stack of paper on his desk. "Grab yourself a cup of coffee—cop coffee, mind you— we don't go in for any of the fancy stuff you bigshots are used to."

"Big shots." Cade laughed out loud. "You got some funny ideas about life in the federal agencies. I'll grab the Joe and be waiting." He strolled from the office.

Gus rolled the plat back up and completed the time-sensitive report he'd been working on. He shuffled the rest of the papers on his desk into a pile. *They'll be here when we get back.*

He met the kid in the break room and refilled his coffee cup. "You got the Jeep. So are you driving or you want me to?"

Cade rose and stretched. "I'm parked right out front. I'll drive, as long as you tell me where to go."

Gus grinned. "One of my specialties."

Laughing, Cade tossed his keys in the air and caught them as they walked to the visitors' parking area. They fastened in and he turned the country station on his radio down low so they could talk on the trip to Azle.

Gus directed him in as they got close. "The shack is about half a mile down the road. Pull over here, through the ditch."

"We going round the back way?" Cade wrestled the wheel as he herded the vehicle through the ditch and came up the other side into a stand of Cottonwood trees.

"Nope. We're hiding this here Jeep and taking Shanks' pony on in."

Cade frowned, then laughed. "Ain't heard that saying since one of my grandpa's old buddies told him he and the wife would be taking it home once the women finished washing dishes."

"Yeah well I may be greying up some but you start calling me grandpa and you'll have a real nice walk back into Fort Worth."

"Yes sir!" Cade grinned and reached for the door handle. "I'll check and make sure we're hid good enough."

Gus grinned and nodded as the kid shut off the Jeep.

They walked quietly following a new fence that encircled the edge of the property. Once they reached the opposite side, they paused.

"Hang on, let me get this apart," Cade stretched the fence as far as he could, and waited while Gus maneuvered his large frame through the opening.

"Thanks. Now see that brush up there about 100 yards? We'll walk that far, and then drop in behind and I'll get into position to give you cover while you get down on your belly and work your way round to that row of buildings."

"Let's hope they don't have any dogs running loose."

"Kelly didn't see any, and I've had a computer tech monitoring the real view images. I suspect that dogs take time and care. From what we've been able to figure out, this location is temporary."

Cade made a face. "Not temporary enough." He released the snap of his holster. "Just in case. I know we're not planning on taking anybody down."

"Not unless we're forced into a showdown. What we want is for you to get up to one of those sheds without being seen, and then figure out how to get a look inside. We need to find out what's stored in there. If it's empty you'll have to check the others, but with a bit of luck you'll get your answers from the first building then we'll get the hell out of here."

"Understood."

Gus handed over a small collar mic and an ear bud. "Put this in your ear and give me a whisper when you're about half way there."

Cade fastened the devices in place. "On my way. You wanna test that out?"

Gus said pointedly, "Don't get caught."

Glancing over his shoulder, Cade grinned. "Read you loud and clear, Chief." He dropped to the ground, rested his weight on his arms and inched along the ground.

Gus watched the agent make his way through the tall fescue, slithering quiet like a snake and moving fast. *Damn good thing I didn't have to join him on this part, they'd have heard me blowing in the next county.* Gus laughed at his own joke.

A minute later, Cade was almost out of sight when he asked, "Yo, Chief. You still got me?"

"All good, be careful now. I see you 'cause I know where to look but they're not going to notice as long as you keep quiet. Easy does it."

"I'm a mouse. Well maybe part rat." Cade chuckled quietly and Gus shook his head. *Damn kids don't take nothing serious.*

After what seemed like an hour but was actually about fifteen minutes, Cade's voice sounded back in Gus' ear.

"We hit the mother lode."

"Well that's something. Okay, get the hell out of there before you draw attention. You can tell me about it when you get back here."

"Can't do that just yet. Hang on, I've got one of them coming."

"Shit."

"Relax. I need to go quiet for a few minutes. Going to move up closer see if I can get a better look. There's something familiar about this dude. Skin head, what looks like a swastika tattooed on his neck, chain swinging from his belt and he seems to be packing a semi."

"Cade you get your ass outta there now." Gus' tirade went unanswered, leaving him with nothing to do but cuss and wait.

Hotheaded young bastards. They're all alike. What the hell's wrong with me, anyhow? I said he reminded me of young Kelly, should have known better than to let him loose. Damn fool's going to get himself killed.

Gus cussed and steamed another five minutes before he let out a final stream of swear words and dropped to the ground.

No way that kid's getting himself offed on my watch. Grimly, moving as quietly as he could through the tall grass, Gus followed the path Cade had made on his way to the sheds.

A shot rang out and Gus froze. His mind raced. *Go on or go back?* He couldn't leave Cade, and if he went back he'd have no idea what was happening. As much as he hated the idea, he pushed ahead.

Another shot, then two more in quick succession. He paused and listened, but there were no voices. No more shots. And when darkness descended and something covered his face, soon there was nothing at all.

Kelly yawned, stretched, and rolled over to glance at the clock. *Ten a.m.* They'd gotten home well after midnight and it was close to two before he'd been able to close his eyes.

Gillian was out the moment her head hit the pillow. He'd considered waking her when he couldn't sleep, but didn't figure that wasn't the smartest way to initiate romance. Now that she'd gotten some rest, waking her seemed like a safer bet.

Laying back the covers, he carefully unbuttoned her red silk pajama top, He loved the fact that she didn't wear the bottoms, only a lacy thong which he had no doubt he could fight his way through.

Her crimson nipples beckoned him, but so did the mysteries hidden under the tiny red thong. He knew how he'd like to be woken up, and smiled when he'd successfully positioned himself between her thighs while rousing her. Using one finger to pull the thong aside, he dipped his tongue between her musky folds and grinned when she jumped.

"Oh, God! Kelly! What are you doing?"

He allowed another languorous lick before replying, "Is that one of those rhetorical questions?"

Her chuckle was sultry and cut off by a gasp when he licked her again. "Um, yeah, I guess so."

Tracing her button-sized nubbin with one thumb, he took another taste. "Did you want me to stop?"

Gillian groaned. "Did you hear me say stop?"

"Nope. I didn't hear you say much of anything coherent."

"Then keep going until you understand exactly what I'm saying."

"Pretty soon here, we won't need words."

She ran her hands through his hair before urging him closer. "I believe we're already to that point, sweetheart."

I truly love this woman. Inhaling to fill his lungs, he buried his face between her legs and gave his tongue free rein to pleasure at will.

Her hips bucked beneath him, and he felt her rise and fall as he sucked intently then backed off. She toyed with his hair until she'd apparently had enough teasing, and grabbed his head when he tried to stop.

"Don't even think about it."

He grinned and dived back in to finish her off.

Gillian cried out as she came, shuddering and shaking. He stayed with her until the intense contractions subsided, then climbed to his knees and drove his hard erection home.

"Oh, God!" Her eyes rolled back in her head. She clutched his shoulders and clung to his neck.

Kelly grasped her deliciously round ass cheeks and pressed deep, desperate to satisfy both of their needs. "Got another one in you?"

"At least."

His grin widened. "My kind of woman. Come on, sugar. I want you to come so hard that I can feel it."

"*You're* so hard." She bit his shoulder lightly. "You fill me up so perfect. It's like we were made for each other."

"I have no doubt that we were. There's nobody but you and me, baby. I love being with you. I love how we complete each other. I love *you*, Gilly McWinter."

She threw her head back and he could feel it when she shattered, more intense that her previous climax. It took all his strength not to explode, but he bit his lip and held back. As soon as he felt her body go limp he drove deep a few more times. He knew every inch of her body by now, and loved how she grew more sensitive with each round. As soon as he was ready, she'd go again.

"Yes!" she called, her voice raspy. "Harder!"

Kelly obliged and within a matter of minutes they were both spiraling over the edge for that final, perfect climax. They gasped and panted and kissed and rolled around on the bed until they finally collapsed in a content, sated heap.

She nuzzled her face against his bare chest. "Damn, baby. That was incredible."

He kissed the top of her head. "Worth waiting for? I mean, our honeymoon was definitely not as promised *or* expected."

Gillian smiled. "It was totally worth waiting for. But now that I know how good it can be, I won't want to wait the next time."

He traced her chin with one finger then lifted her face to his for a kiss. "You don't have to wait. Anything you want, anytime you want it. I'm right here, love. I learned my lesson about combining business with pleasure because it doesn't work."

"It sounded like a good plan," she agreed. "But now we know. Be wary of Stella's bright ideas."

He laughed. "We shouldn't have any more worries where Marcy is concerned. With Spadina still out there, Mark hired his own team to guard her 'round the clock. She's gonna hate that."

"She's gonna *totally* hate that," Gillian agreed. "But she's back with her family, and she doesn't plan on working much with the baby coming, so she'll be fine. Having a bodyguard isn't the worst thing in the world." She circled his flat nipple with the palm of her hand, then leaned in and sucked the bud until it peaked.

He sighed his pleasure and she did it again.

"Really?" Kelly raised his eyebrows.

She grinned. "Turnabout is fair play." Gillian slipped under the covers and settled between his legs.

She'd just gotten started when his phone rang.

"No way!" he yelled.

Gillian voice sounded muffled with her mouth full. "Answer it if you want, but I'm not stopping."

"Of course I don't want to answer it." He couldn't resist lifting the cell to read the caller ID. *Gus.* "Fuck."

She increased her suction and repeated, "Answer if you want."

He ran his hands over her head. "I don't even hear it ringing."

Gillian chuckled but kept going. The phone silenced, then the notification light began to blink with the voicemail.

Kelly closed his eyes, trying to ignore it.

"Was it Gus?" she mumbled.

"I didn't take the call, remember?" He jerked his hips.

Her tone remained amused. "It was probably very important."

He lifted the covers to look at her. "You sure are chatty. Are you going to keep talking? Just so I can be prepared mentally."

Gillian threw back the sheet and rose above him with a wicked grin. "Prepare yourself for this, lover." She impaled herself on his shaft, pressing on his solid stomach as she rose and fell.

"Aw, shit." He couldn't believe he was so close again that fast, but the sight of her breasts bobbing in the air always did him in. "You know I love that."

She eyed him seductively. "Come on, stud. Show me what you got."

"Mmm, I can see what you've got, and I like it. Aw, hell, I love it. I love you." He groaned and succumbed to the climax that overtook him without much warning.

Bouncing above him, she released a low-keening wail as she came, plying him with the perfect balance of give and take.

She finally collapsed on top of him, both of them gasping for air.

When their mouths found each other they kissed, tongues battling for dominance. To Kelly's amazement, his shaft had only been out a couple of minutes when it hardened again.

She felt it pressing against her belly and growled into his mouth as they kissed. It was the sexiest sound he thought he'd ever heard. He ran his hands over her sweat-slicked skin, down her sides and cupped her ass. "Again?" he whispered, his voice hoarse.

"Oh, yes. Take me from behind this time."

"Damn," he swore, both shocked and thrilled that their intense love-making session was continuing.

His phone rang again, and they both froze.

Gillian was on all fours, glancing back over her shoulder at him.

The sight of her perfect, glistening ass was nearly more than he could bear. "Ignore it."

She reached for the cell and looked at the screen. "It's Gus. Are you sure you should?"

He lined a trail of warm kisses along her spine, then rested his forehead against her shoulder blade. "Fuck!"

Gillian pressed the talk button. "Hello. Oh, hi, Gus. No, he's not busy, just feeding Jake. Hold on, he'll be right here." She smiled as she handed the phone over.

More disappointed than he ever remembered being, Kelly snatched the phone. "Yep?"

"Hey, buddy. Sorry to keep pestering you but we've got us a situation in Azle and I need to brief you on it."

Kelly sighed. "I don't suppose it could wait a half an hour or so."

"It really shouldn't. The ATF is sending a team from the Dallas field office, and they'll be here soon. I'd like you in on that meeting. Actually, I'd like you here beforehand so I can fill you in on recent developments."

"I'll be there as soon as I can." His reply came out gruffer than he'd intended.

Gus sounded confused. "Is Jake okay?"

"Jake's fine. I'll see you in a few." He ended the call and gave one last, longing look at the beautiful ass before him. "Maybe if we hurry?" He gazed at her pleadingly.

Gillian laughed. "You know what, sugar? I'm not sure I want to hurry. Why don't you go do whatever it is that Gus needs you to do. I'll check on the horses and the kids out at the stables. And whenever we're both done, we'll pick up right where we left off."

He ran a hand over one firm ass cheek. "You promise? Because looking at this beautiful booty gave a whole new meaning to third time's a charm."

Her grin widened. "I promise. I don't know what got into you today but I like it. Scratch that, *I love it.* And I'll expect more of the same ASAP. Deal?"

"Deal." Kelly placed light kisses on each of her cheeks then dragged himself off to the shower. He didn't wait for it to warm up. Today, he needed it cold.

Chapter Ten

Kelly poured himself a cup of coffee and sipped it in the hall outside of Gus' office. He could see the chief was on the phone, and Gus had held up one finger indicating he should wait. As soon as the called ended, Gus waved him in.

"Welcome back. How was the Vegas?"

Sidetracked remembering the morning rather than the previous few days, Kelly smiled. "Great." He shook his head to clear it. "Well, Vegas was horrible, and so was LA. But everything else was great."

Gus chuckled. "Some honeymoon, huh? And Spadina is still at large?"

"Yes, but he's now the problem of the security agency Mark Fisher hired to protect his wife and her relatives. Marcy's happily ensconced on her family's ranch back in Tennessee. She'll be fine." He moved around the desk and noticed some fresh, red scratches on the side of Gus' face. "What the devil happened to you?"

A dark-haired man wearing a plaid shirt and jeans bustled into the office without knocking and approached the desk, a sleek, silver laptop in hand. "Wait 'til you see what I found."

Kelly studied him for a moment then glanced at Gus, who didn't seem put out that the man had just invited himself in. "Excuse me?" He turned to Gus. "And you were just getting ready to tell me what the hell happened to you?"

Gus waved a hand. "Easy, boy. Kelly McWinter, this is Cade Wyatt, Special Agent with the ATF. Cade, Kelly is the PI I've been telling you about."

Cade set the computer on Gus' desk and extended a hand to shake. "Kelly, glad to meet you. Gus speaks highly of you."

Kelly shook hands and examined the man at the same time. Tall, maybe an inch shorter than him, with messy hair and beard scruff. "Special Agent, huh? No offense, kid, but you don't look like any fed I've ever seen."

"None taken. You were expecting a balding, middle-aged man with a pot belly?"

"Hey now," Gus muttered.

Kelly allowed a small smile. "To tell the truth, I wasn't expecting anyone. Gus said the ATF was coming in from Dallas later, and he wanted to speak with me before they got here. Something about recent developments?"

Gus motioned to one of the two chairs in front of his desk. "Sit down and we'll fill you in. Cade came by earlier. His bureau sent him down to check out our situation. They weren't too concerned and figured it was a one man job."

Kelly sat and watched the agent make himself comfortable in the other chair. He turned his laptop around so they could see the screen. "And did they ever figure wrong. See, Gus and I took a run out to Azle this morning. There's more going on out there than any of us knew. Check this out." He pointed to a live action satellite image on screen. "This is the Clements' ranch. Look over here, Gus. A dog pen. They have at least six big old brutes. Not sure if that's counting the one I had to subdue this morning." He raised his eyebrows. "Guess we should have checked this before we went, and not relied on the images you'd had printed off."

Gus waved his hand. "Damn technology. Just when I think I know what intel we're capable of getting everything changes. I can barely keep up."

Settling back into the chair, Kelly folded his arms across his chest. "So knowing that, the two of you took off to Azle alone to confront God knows who, or what, you might have found out there?"

The chief gazed at him evenly. "Well there was two of us, so we weren't exactly alone. And we didn't go to confront anybody. I wanted Cade to get a look at the place so we could start getting the lay of the land. There's more than a shack out there, Kelly, lots more. The main house is set way back. There are bunkhouses and sheds, military Humvees and barbwire fences."

"I suspected as much when I saw the troops with the assault rifles. This is out of our wheelhouse, Gus. That's why I asked you to call in the big boys. I just didn't realize they'd be sending Opie Taylor with a pistol and a bullet in his pocket."

Cade grinned. "It was Barney Fife who had the pistol and had to keep the bullet in his pocket. Course we'll never know what happened to Opie, but I suspect he grew up to be a tall and very well respected man."

"You're tall enough," Kelly conceded. "Are you well respected, Agent Wyatt?"

"Special Agent." Cade chuckled. "And I guess that depends who you talk to. Ask my mama, hell yeah. Everyone in Denton, Texas has heard of me. Can't go to the Piggly Wiggly or the Dairy Queen without running into someone who knows that federal lawman, Peggy Wyatt's boy. Now, ask my boss or the Director of my bureau and you might get another story. I tend to run on the ornery side, and don't generally like to bother with the red tape of bureaucracy. They hate that about me. But I'm good at my job and I'm a crack shot, so they keep me around, much as it pains them sometimes."

Kelly didn't know how to respond to the man so he turned to Gus instead. "What happened in Azle this morning?"

"Cade skirted under a fence to get inside for a better look around. He spotted someone and had to go radio silent. I heard gunshots and when I couldn't raise Cade I went in after him. Stupidly, I guess, because the only thing I encountered was approximately one hundred pounds of some type of pit bull mix. He wasn't happy to see me. Knocked me down and damned near knocked me out. Lucky for me, Cade came back and bagged the bugger in an old gunnysack he found. We tied the bag and got the hell outta there before he could chew his way free. But not before Cade got a look at what those boys are storing in their sheds."

Kelly shook his head in disbelief. "What about the shots?"

"Hmm?" Gus blinked.

"You said you heard gunshots."

Cade smiled sheepishly. "The guy I spotted was attempting to pick off squirrels. Lucky for the rodents he was a lousy shot. Don't think he even grazed one."

Kelly closed his eyes. "I can't believe you two."

Gus chuckled. "Wait 'til you hear the rest. Tell him what you found, Cade."

Not sure he wanted to know, Kelly glanced at the agent warily.

"Assault rifles. Cases and cases of them. More than they need in that little setup of theirs."

Gus interrupted. "So they're either selling them, or stocking up for a war. Neither of which is allowed in my little corner of Texas."

Inhaling to calm himself, Kelly exhaled slowly and chose his words carefully. "You two know how lucky you are, don't you?"

Gus blinked. "What? This isn't my first rodeo. And even though he looks twelve, the kid here knows his stuff. We got the info we went out there for."

"And you immediately came back and called the ATF, right? So you can turn this over to them and bow out?"

"Well..." Gus made a face. "It's slightly more complicated that that."

Cade leaned forward. "The Director is sending a team, yes. The ATF is very interested in the compound and the weapons. They believe what you've got here is a new chapter of the Western American Militia, a homegrown terrorist organization. We've seen groups springing up all over the Midwest and Southwest in recent months and years. To get a foothold, these people look for rural, secluded areas with enough land that their training activities will go unnoticed. States with open carry laws are particularly attractive, and as you know Texas doesn't have a ban on assault weapons."

Kelly gazed at him. "But we frown on the sale of them to bat-shit crazy militants."

"There is that," Cade acknowledged. "The team will monitor the ranch for a few days or weeks, as long as necessary to establish illegal activities."

"You're saying the ATF is just gonna sit and watch?"

Cade shrugged. "It's not against the law for them to be there. We just have to find out whatever it is they're actually doing. Shouldn't take long. You get that many miscreants in one place and pretty soon someone's going to do something wrong. At that point we can take them down, disassemble the group and send the worst ones away for some federally sponsored R&R."

"And the others will move on to set up shop somewhere else." Kelly had no delusions. People like that weren't easily dissuaded from their causes.

"As long as they're out of my county," Gus agreed. "We'll just hope we can put away the biggest fish, and maybe the smaller fries will get bored playing army and move on to some new pastime."

"Yeah like strapping explosives on their backs and blowing up airports." Kelly narrowed his eyes and looked at Cade. "The ATF has a plan. Good deal. I wish you boys the best of luck. So Gus, what do you have to do? Find them some office space, a place for them to hang their hats?"

Cade answered for him. "It's a little more complicated than that. The bureau relies pretty heavily on local law enforcement to assist with their investigations. We have no illusions, these guys know the area far better than we do, even with the technology at our fingertips. The other part of that equation is a bit more personal."

Kelly blinked. "Meaning?"

Gus cleared his throat. "Meaning these are my people, Kelly. Yours and mine. The feds don't give a shit about the three boys who've gone missing. Me on the other hand, I've got three families calling me every day for updates, with very little I can tell them at this point. We have no direct proof that links the kids to whatever the fuck is going on at the Clements' ranch. But given the military tie-ins we've established, and Wade Clements suddenly going AWOL on a pretty sweet probation gig, I think we all know where those kids are."

Rubbing his chin, Kelly mulled over what Gus said. "You think Wade is luring them in, like some modern day Pied Piper?"

Gus nodded. "That's how these groups get members. But those boys are too young. If there's even the slightest chance they aren't there willingly, we need to know about that, too."

Kelly still wasn't convinced. "I can't vouch for the intelligence of Wade Clements, but the kid was smart enough to hack into a government computer system so he has to have a few brains. If he's running from his probation officer, wouldn't you think he'd scoot a little farther from home? I mean, somebody checked there, right? If the ranch is his parents' legal residence, then law enforcement has the right to knock on the door and ask if little Wade is home and can come out to play."

Gus shuffled papers on his desk and read from one of them. "The PO's report says the parents haven't lived there in a number of years. They have a place in town, which Wade listed as his permanent address. Yes, someone checked there and no, Wade couldn't come out to play."

"Or wouldn't," Kelly mused. He glanced from one man to the other. "Bottom line, what's the ATF need, and who are they figuring's going to give it to them?"

Gus answered before Cade could. "I'm establishing a task force, but as you well know my manpower is limited. I want you with us on this, Kelly. I can't say exactly what 'this' is, until we've had a chance to discuss the particulars with the ATF team. I'm sure they'll have some kind of plan."

Kelly made a face. He knew without even bouncing it off her that his wife wouldn't like this assignment one bit. He wasn't keen on it himself, but he respected and trusted Gus immensely. When the chief needed him, he made it a point to be there. But he had to be honest. "Can't say I like the sounds of it that much. I *can* say I know for certain Gillian won't like it."

Cade raised his eyebrows. "Gillian?"

"My wife."

The agent glanced at Gus.

"Newlyweds," the chief offered by way of explanation.

Cade nodded. "Ah, gotcha. I was married once for about five minutes. My wife never had a say in my cases."

Kelly smiled grimly. "Which might explain the five minute business. I don't work for the Fort Worth Police Department anymore, Special Agent Wyatt. I put in thirteen years before my first wife was blown up because of my activities involving taking down a meth lab. I should have been with her that night, and for many years after I wished I had been. It took a long time, but I eventually found some peace and got my life back."

A look of horror crossed Cade's face. "I'm sorry. I didn't mean to get personal."

Kelly went on without a flicker of emotion. "Of course you didn't. I don't tell that story to very many people. I'm telling it to you now to make things clear. I work for myself these days. I consider Gus a trusted friend and I appreciate the jobs he sends my way. But Gillian is the most important person in my life, and I will consider her before accepting any cases."

"Understood and again, I'm sorry if I crossed a line. I'd have to agree with Gus, though. We could really use you on this task force. Lawmen with the right balance of brains, bravado, knowledge and experience are hard to come by."

Kelly couldn't help but chuckle. "Were you describing me just then, or yourself?"

Cade grinned. "It's like looking in a mirror, isn't it?"

Gus rubbed his temples. "Lord, help me."

* * *

Stella met Gillian at the front door of the Hideaway and hugged her so tight Gillian thought she might break a rib. "Oh my God, Gill, I thought you'd never get out here."

"Well, thanks. It's good to be missed."

"Oh, you know what I mean. We were on pins and needles when we heard about Rachel being kidnapped out in California. We didn't really know what had happened. Gus didn't give us any details, just said Marcy's sister had been kidnapped and Kelly was dealing with it. For all I knew they might have snatched all of you."

"We're fine, Stella." Gillian squirmed a bit.

Stella released her hold. "I know you called last week and said you'd be by as soon as you could, but you know what I'm like."

"I really am sorry it took me so long to get out here. I just haven't had a minute to myself since we got back."

"I'm not trying to make you feel guilty. I've just been a bit bored lately. Having you come by and tell me all the latest news is the most exciting thing that's happened since Ethel got sick of Doug spending every day playing crib with Frank and not getting any chores done. She charged in here, grabbed him by the ear and yanked him squealing out the door."

"Oh, she did not."

"Yes, she did. Honest to God. Must have worked it out though—or at least he got the chores done—cause as you can see they're right back at it again." Stella waved towards the back of the room, where two old men sat hunched over a cribbage board with a pot of coffee between them.

"I don't know what those old timers would do if you and Cam didn't keep the Hideaway open every day and supply them with bottomless cups of coffee."

"I know. To tell you the truth we really shouldn't even be open during the day. Cam only cranks the barbecue up to prep for the dinner hour, but he just doesn't have the heart to shut this place down in the daytime."

"Kind of rough on the two of you with him working nights and you working days."

"Well, that's going to come to an end this fall. I don't mind helping out while Cam gets new wait staff trained, but as you well know I'm not temperamentally, or intellectually, fit for a lifetime of bartending." Stella grinned.

Gillian nodded her head in agreement. "So what are you going to do?"

"Oh no." Stella shook her head. "You're not getting me off topic by talking about me and my plans. I want to hear all about your trip, and don't you dare leave out any details."

"Okay, you've got yourself a deal, but how about if we go sit down?"

Stella threw her hands up in the air. "I do not know what is wrong with me, I guess I'm just so happy to see you I've forgotten any manners I ever had. Come on, let's go sit at the bar. I'll get you a coffee and if anyone else comes in here I'll holler at Frank to take care of them."

Stella headed towards the bar at the front of the room and waited impatiently while Gillian stopped to say a word to Frank Perkins and Doug Phillips.

"Say what've you done with old Kelly? We practically ain't seen that boy since the two of you got hitched. You ain't got him tied up to the apron strings now, do ya?" Frank winked at Gillian like they shared an old joke. "Tell him hey for me."

Gillian played along and promised to pass the word on, before moving to the bar with Stella.

"Not much changed around here as you can see." Stella set a cup of coffee in front of Gillian and leaned her elbows on the bar. "I'm just so glad you're all okay. I've talked to Marcy nearly every day. She's doing well, and the baby seems fine."

"Good. Did Rachel go back to school?"

"Yep. *Kids*. The girl got kidnapped, met some of the biggest names in country music, then went right back to school and started complaining about a paper that's due."

Gillian laughed. "Good thing they're so resilient. It's taken me a week to get rested up. It was a few stressful days."

Stella frowned. "I can only imagine. I want to hear all about it, good and bad. Now tell me everything. The kidnapping, how many stars you saw, the trip to Vegas, and don't leave out anything about the awards. Did you see Blake Shelton?"

That took the next hour and a half. Gillian's explanations and descriptions were regularly punctuated by Stella's gasps and ooohs and aaahs.

Finally, after finishing her third cup of coffee and feeling pretty much talked out, Gillian reached for a bag she'd placed on the floor beside her and handed it over to Stella.

"This is a small thank you for the gown you gave me, with my sincerest appreciation. It was wonderful, and I might add, even garnered me a compliment from Blake Shelton himself."

"Wow! What about your husband?"

"Oh, I'll just say that he loved the dress, but I must admit what he loved the most was getting me out of it at the end of the evening.”

“Okay, you can leave the rest to my imagination. As you know, I’ve got a good one.”

Gillian laughed. “Like I said, I’m ever so grateful, and this is just a little thank you.”

“You know how much I love surprises.” Stella dug into the bag and came up with a square white box, with black lettering and a distinctive pink ribbon.

“You didn’t.”

Gillian smiled and nodded as Stella tore open the box and pulled out a very sexy black satin and lace nightgown.

“Oh, boy. Wait till Cam gets a load of me in this.” She held the sheer gown close to her chest to keep the prying eyes at the back of the room from viewing her prize.

“He’ll love getting you out of it, you mean.”

Stella stroked the smooth fabric and winked. “You said it, sister, and by the way, what about those pictures you promised to bring back.”

“Oh, I got them. Don’t you worry. I’ve just got to get them out of the camera and drop them off to get developed. I could have used my cell phone, but hey, this was supposed to be my honeymoon, I wanted good pictures.”

“I hope you weren’t too disappointed at the way your honeymoon turned out.”

Gillian chuckled. "Don't you believe it. I had the time of my life, and you better believe we managed to squeeze some mighty sexy honeymoon stuff, in between the kidnappings and shooting and celebrity mashing."

Stella grinned. "If you don't look every bit like the cat that swallowed the canary I don't know who does."

"Guilty. I've got to get back now, but next time we get together I'll tell you all about a little place that Kelly found where they sell cupcakes with names like "Better Than Sex".

Chapter Eleven

Kelly paced around the conference room Gus had set up as home base for the Clements' Ranch task force. He paused in front of the large bulletin board, loaded with clippings and photos.

Cade joined him with two cups of coffee. "Black, right?"

"Thanks." Kelly nodded and accepted the cup. "I'm trying to figure out what these people are thinking. If they have the three boys, they have to know the kids are underage, and someone is bound to come looking for them."

Cade shrugged. "Groups such as WAM like to get the kids young and mold them just the way they want. I've seen ten year olds brought up in the ranks and it's a scary sight. I saw one kid that age who was probably a better shot than me."

"That is scary. Kids should be kids, right? I mean, I never had any, but it seems like they need time to play and have fun before they have to get into real world stuff."

"I suspect some of these A-holes think shooting assault rifles *is* fun. I'd rather have my kids chasing virtual Pokémon."

Kelly laughed. "Oh now, come on! Not video games. Kids need to get dirty, play baseball, football, that kind of stuff."

Cade grinned. "I can play those games on my phone, man. But, I know what you mean. There's nothing inherently wrong with computers and video games. It's all about finding balance, and moderation in everything."

Nodding, Kelly had to agree. The kid made sense, and he found himself liking the guy more each time they talked. Something he said made Kelly wonder and he had to ask, "So, do *you* have kids?"

"Me? No way! The former Mrs. Wyatt and I talked about it, but she insisted that having children required a maturity that I apparently lacked. I replied by sticking my tongue out at her and making armpit noises."

Kelly didn't want to laugh but he couldn't help himself. He shook his head. "Okay, you just said something about your kids chasing Pokémon."

"You caught me, I was talking about myself. I'm on level fifteen and actually stuck right now."

Two other members of the ATF approached the table and Kelly lowered his voice to warn Cade. "For future reference, that's the last conversation I want to have about anything to do with Pokémon. *Capisce?*"

"Got ya." He turned to the two agents. "Morning Jim, Steve."

Steve Brock was the senior agent on the case, a tall stocky man with a bright red crew cut. "Morning gentlemen. We finally have word from the Deputy Director on the direction of our investigation. Once Chief Graham gets here we'll brief you."

Jim Pace took a seat at the big conference room table and sipped from a Grande-sized Starbucks cup. "You're gonna love it." His sly grin showed pearly white teeth in contrast to his dark skin.

Kelly rubbed his chin and turned to Cade. "Not sure I like his expression."

Cade chuckled. "That's a shit-eating grin if I've ever seen one."

Gus lumbered in and settled his frame into the big chair at the end of the table. "Y'all ready to get started?"

"I'll reserve comment." Kelly rolled his eyes at Cade and they each took a seat.

Brock opened a folder and began the briefing. "The Deputy Director has decided the best way to infiltrate the Clements' ranch is to send a couple of people in undercover. We already have a man entrenched in another chapter of WAM, he's been under for a year and a half, so he'll be a good one to vouch for our new arrivals."

All eyes turned to Cade, and Kelly had the urge to squirm. "Why do I get the feeling you're up to your neck in this?"

Cade grinned. "I love undercover work. Are we going in? How soon can we get started?"

Brock rolled his eyes. "Hold your horses, cowboy. We figure it'll take at least three days for you to get your story memorized. We're thinking you'll go in as brothers, members of a white supremacist organization. Kelly will have done some time in Huntsville. You'll both need a couple of tattoos. Really obnoxious ones, like swastikas. You don't have much credibility with these people unless you have visible tats."

"Right here." Cade pointed to the base of Kelly's neck. "That'll look *awesome*."

Kelly blinked. "How do you plan to pull that off? Rub-ons from Cracker Jacks?"

Pace chuckled. "We have an artist who uses ink. It won't rinse away if you get caught in the rain, but it can be scrubbed off. Unless you decide to take one for the team, and just go ahead and have the real things done."

Heaving a sigh, Kelly replied, "As appealing as a swastika on the neck sounds, we're not getting tattoos." He glanced at Cade, who seemed way more into the undercover assignment than Kelly did. "Course maybe I shouldn't speak for you."

"Eh, you're probably right. My poor ol' mom already had one stroke. I don't need to give her another."

"For real?" Kelly was surprised. He was just starting to get to know Cade, but the kid was full of surprises.

"Oh yeah. She's doing okay, now. Has my dad to look out for her. I try to see her when I can. The stroke was a wake-up call for all of us. Life is short, man."

Brock coughed. "Sorry about your mom, but can we get back on task, here? We've got three days to set up this operation and we need you two to be fool-proof."

Kelly frowned. "I'm sorry, but I see one problem with this plan. Nobody asked me if I minded going undercover. I've already told Cade, and I'll tell you guys. I don't work for the Fort Worth PD. My participation is strictly by choice, and I'm not sure this is something I want to do."

Pace replied, "The ATF will bump your pay, if that helps. It'll be a considerable bump."

"For a considerable amount of danger, it should be. But it's not about the money. I'm just not sure I want to get involved in this mess." *And Gillian will have my hide.*

Gus rose and removed three photos from the bulletin board. He set them down on the table in front of Kelly. "I can't make you do this, friend. Only you can make that call. But remember who we're doing it for." He tapped each photo as he said the names. "Isaiah West. Stuart Falkner. Ben Lehman. Fifteen and sixteen years old. They may have joined this 'WAM' group willingly, but if they change their minds and decide they want to go home, we all know getting out won't be so easy. These boys are in trouble, Kelly. Kids from right here in Fort Worth, Ben is even from the Indian Creek area. These are our kids. We need to help them if we can."

Kelly tapped the photo of dark-skinned Isaiah West. "This one doesn't fit. A white supremacist group isn't going to recruit a black kid."

"Maybe not, but the timing of his disappearance is suspect."

Sighing, Kelly rubbed his temples. "I know, damn it."

* * *

Gillian leaned up against the wall of the FWPD conference room, watching a buxom blonde makeup artist by the name of Brandi ink a thick, black swastika on Kelly's Adam's apple. The process didn't appear to hurt, but it made Gill mighty damned uncomfortable. "That's gonna come off, right?"

"Eventually." Brandi worked as she spoke. "The ink is semi-permanent, which means it'll take a lot of scrubbing."

"Sounds painful." Gillian made a face. She wasn't happy *at all* about Kelly's undercover gig, and he knew it. Hell, according to him, he knew she wouldn't like

199

it before he even took the job. Yet something about the case struck a nerve with her husband, and he was determined to follow through with the assignment. She hadn't seriously tried to talk him out of it because she'd never interfere, and she trusted his gut instincts. But watching him get the ink made it somehow more real, and strangely sinister. Her stomach turned and she shivered as the process continued.

Brandi finished the swastika and showed Kelly a couple more designs. "The Texas Brotherhood logo on your upper arm would look good. It'd be more visible on one of your hands or forearms, but those are riskier choices because you'll wash your hands more frequently, and the ink will fade."

"Upper arm is fine." He removed his button-down plaid shirt and rolled up the edge of his T-shirt sleeve to give her better access.

"Go ahead and sit." Brandi motioned to a chair. "I've got a stencil for this one, it won't take long." She sat next to him and when she turned to gather her supplies, her breasts brushed his arm.

Kelly glanced away, obviously trying to look anywhere but at her barely concealed cleavage.

Gillian would have laughed if it hadn't been so blasted hot in the room. The lack of air was stifling. For a moment, she thought she might pass out. She reached out for the nearest chair and dropped into it.

Gus gazed at her. "You okay? You're pale as the ghost of the Fort Worth Zoo."

Brandi stopped what she was doing and glanced at Gus. "What ghost?"

He grinned and leaned forward in his chair. "We have a couple, actually. A trainer crushed in an accident is s'posed to haunt the elephant and zebra areas. But the more intriguing one is the woman in a white, old fashioned dress who paces in front of the zoo's café."

Kelly nodded. "They say she carries a parasol and appears very forlorn."

Cade, studying his own neck tattoo in a mirror, cackled. "You don't believe that?"

"I didn't say I believed it. I just repeated what I've heard." Kelly was still trying to look anywhere but at Brandi's chest. He glanced at Gillian. "You do look pale. These will wash off, babe. You know I wouldn't be doing it if I wasn't sure of that."

She offered a half-hearted smile. "I know. It's just warm in here. I'm going to use the ladies room." Rising, she paused for a moment to steady herself before taking a step.

Kelly started to bolt forward. "Are you all right?"

"Hey! Hold still," Brandi admonished.

Gillian smiled apologetically. "I'm sorry, I'm in the way. I thought it'd be fun to see how she did the artwork, but I should go."

Trying hard not to move much, Kelly reached out his opposite hand and grabbed Gillian. "You can stay. You're not in the way."

She leaned down and pressed a quick kiss on his mouth. "You're sweet, but I'm going. I'll see you tonight. One last home cooked meal before you go undercover."

He squeezed her hand and his gaze held hers. "This'll be fine. If all goes well we may only have to be there a few days."

Gillian nodded. "It's okay, sugar. I'll see you soon." Her head was spinning and she really just wanted to go. Shooting him a reassuring wink, she hurried out to the hallway and darted into the nearest restroom. She barely made it into the stall before losing her lunch and some of her breakfast.

Standing in front of the sink, she dampened a paper towel and wiped her face, then held it to her forehead. "What the—?" *I never get sick.* Kelly's case was weighing on her mind, but she hadn't realized how much. The group he was infiltrating contained a bunch of crazy, dangerous, heavily armed men. *Not a good combination.*

She leaned against the sink and studied her reflection. *Kelly knows what he's doing.* He'd never been one to take foolish chances. And Cade seemed to be a competent guy. *Young.* He hadn't bothered to avert his eyes when Brandi applied his tattoos. He flirted up a storm with the pretty girl. Gillian wouldn't be surprised if Cade's last evening before going under involved something to do with Brandi. He seemed every bit the playboy, but not stupid. Hopefully smart enough not to pick up a stranger while he was decked out with white supremacist tattoos.

She steadied herself, making sure she was okay for the drive home.

Breathe.

The cool towel helped, and after a few minutes, Gillian felt better. She wanted to get out of there before another wave hit. Judging from the way her stomach gurgled, that scenario was a matter of 'when' and not 'if'.

She made it home before getting sick again, then crawled into bed hoping a short nap would rejuvenate her. Jake nuzzled her hand hanging off the side of the bed for a few minutes, then curled up on the floor and dozed off. Gillian closed her eyes, willing the nausea to pass.

When she opened her eyes again, the sun was setting and the room dark. "Oh, crap!" She sat up and wiped her eyes, trying to get her bearings. She'd intended to make a special dinner for Kelly and now it was evening and she hadn't even thought about it again.

Hurrying to the bathroom she washed up, relieved that she actually felt better. Her mind raced over what food she had in the house and how she could make a wonderful meal out of it. She headed to the kitchen and realized from the smell of garlic and something cheesy someone beat her there.

Kelly was leaning over the oven, checking on a foil-wrapped pan.

Confused and mortified she'd slept all afternoon, she almost couldn't face him. "Hey," she said softly.

He stood and smiled. "Well hey there, Sleeping Beauty." He closed the oven door. "You okay?"

"God, Kelly, I'm so sorry! I had grand plans to fix you something really special tonight."

"Didn't you get my text?"

She shook her head. "I'm afraid I haven't checked my phone. I was just so tired all of a sudden."

He cupped her waist and pulled her toward him. "I got that impression. I know it's been a stressful few weeks, babe. The honeymoon that was supposed to be fun went downhill fast—"

"It was fun, Kelly."

"Except for the kidnappings and the armed gunmen, yeah, I know. And I still owe you a vacation. That's not lost on me. I just need to finish this thing I started with Gus. I think we'll both be able to relax once this case is resolved."

She shot him a skeptical look. "Until the next case, you mean."

A guilty expression crossed his face. "Gill..."

She smiled and shook her head. "Don't say it. I knew what I was getting into when I married at PI. Well, I thought I knew. I haft'a admit it's been a little hairier than I expected lately, but I trust you, sugar. I have every confidence you know what you're doing."

His worried look morphed into one of his gorgeous smiles. "Have I told you lately that I love you?"

Gillian cupped his face with both hands. "Not for at least eight hours, and that's a damn long time. I love you too. And when you look at me like that—whew! Somebody break out the hose to cool me off."

Laughing now, he drew her close and kissed her neck. "I don't want to cool you off. I like you hot and bothered. I also like you out of those clothes, but full disclosure, I have pasta and garlic bread from Portelli's warming in the oven. That's what my text was about. So do you want to eat first, or—?"

She reached for his belt buckle. "Definitely 'or'. The food smells divine but I've got my favorite thing right here in my arms."

He nuzzled her neck. "You love Portelli's pasta."

Gillian untucked his shirt and ran her hands up the bare skin on his back. "I love you more." Face to face with the swastika, she gulped. "I don't love this phony tat, but I can put it out of my mind for one night."

Kelly nibbled her earlobe. "Please don't ever put *me* out of your mind."

Her heart melted. "I never have, since the day we met. You're part of me, Kelly McWinter. One of the best parts of me."

Still teasing her ear with his tongue, he walked her backwards to the bedroom. "Seems what we have here is a mutual admiration society. Because I think you're the best part of me, Gillian McWinter. And you are never out of my mind, or my heart."

They undressed each other before hitting the mattress where he flipped her onto her stomach and raised her hips.

Smiling, she gazed at him over her shoulder. "That's how it's gonna be, huh?"

He winked. "As much as you hate looking at these tattoos, I hate the idea that you'll associate them with our love-making. This way you won't have to see them, yet we both get what we want. A win-win situation."

She gasped when he took her with one smooth thrust. Clutching the sheets, she rocked in rhythm with his body, until they were both sweaty and panting. "Aw, lordy!" Her voice sounded breathy to her own ears.

Kelly kissed her back but didn't slow his motions. "Bring it home, sugar." His right hand snaked between her legs and he cupped her, then circled her clit with his thumb.

"That's gonna do it," she warned, her climax beckoning.

"I'm right there with ya." His words were staccato, through gritted teeth.

When he hit just the right spot, she shattered. Her growl gave her away, and somewhere in her subconscious mind she could tell he'd joined her. She held on, trying to remain upright, as he clutched her hips for the final few thrusts.

They came to a stop and Kelly circled an arm around her stomach and settled them on their sides in the bed. Kissing her arm and shoulder, wherever he could reach, he murmured sweet words that were music to her ears.

She turned her head and captured his mouth in a long, wet kiss.

"Thank you," he finally murmured once they'd caught their breath.

"Thank *you*." She crinkled her eyes at him. "You make me feel so special and loved."

"You are special and loved. It's my job to remind you of that. You're just gonna have to remember for the next few days, though. It won't be safe for me to call you. Gus can keep you apprised of everything that's happening. And as soon as we can bring some closure to this thing I'll be outta there, and right back here with you."

"Promise?"

"You know I do."

A stab of fear jolted her and Gillian grabbed his face. "I mean it, Kelly, Promise me."

He caressed her cheek. "I'll be home soon. *I promise*. With all my heart." He kissed her again.

Gillian held tight, never wanting the moment to end.

Chapter Twelve

Kelly stepped out of Cade's Jeep and followed him around to the front of the vehicle. "This is some privacy fence." The property line of the Clements' ranch was protected by an eight-foot high barricade, which appeared to be electrically charged.

Cade looked up at the three rows of barbed wire lining the top. "For anyone who's not put off by the electric current."

"You can't fix stupid."

"No, but you can shock the hell out of it."

The click of a gun being cocked caught their attention, and Kelly spotted a rifle barrel poking out through the fence. "Three o'clock," he muttered under his breath.

Frozen in place, Cade followed his gaze then whispered, "Noted. It would appear the current isn't flowing."

Unmoving, Kelly scanned the fence for anyone else but could only see the one gunman. Still speaking in hushed tones he added, "Which is not to say it won't be the next time. So don't take chances."

"Yep." Cade twirled the toothpick poking out from between his front teeth with his tongue.

The man behind the fence finally spoke, his voice twangy. "Appears you boys got the wrong *add*-ress. I'd get back in my car and keep going if I was you."

Kelly rubbed the scruff on his chin. Several retorts buzzed though his mind, but he knew this wasn't the time. *I suspect we'll be putting up with a lot more redneck BS before we're done here.* He bit his tongue and stayed on task. "We're looking for Boyd Bennett."

"Nobody here by that name."

"Really? Cause he's expecting us. Jesse Crawford told him we'd be showing up."

The man peered through the fence at each of them, then pulled the gun out. "Just wait right there. Either one of you does something stupid it'll be the last time. We don't shoot to scare around here."

"Understood." Kelly glanced at Cade and they waited, stock-still, for the man to check their story.

He returned a few minutes later and unlocked the fence, then motioned for them to come in. "We can take you to the office, but I need to check you for weapons. Either of you armed?"

Kelly shook his head and raised his hands shoulder height so the man could frisk him.

Cade did the same, adding, "There's a sawed-off under the front seat of the Jeep."

The stocky guy in a stained T-shirt and ratty jeans frisked Cade then searched the

Jeep, removing the shotgun. He looked in the back and, apparently satisfied he'd found all their weapons, nodded toward an old red Ford pickup.

"Pull your Jeep in and follow that truck right there. About a half mile down the road you'll see where to park. Sparky will take you to the office."

Kelly nodded and returned to the Jeep. They climbed in and Cade did as directed, trailing the well-worn, rusted Ford.

The first man secured the gate behind them and remained at his post.

Cade's gaze darted in all directions as he drove. "Sparky, huh? Could this place get any more redneck?"

"I had the same thought earlier. Didn't think it'd be wise to speak it aloud." Kelly glanced around, soaking up as much information as he could as they bumped down the dirt path.

"Doubt these boys would take too kindly to our observations. Here we go."

The driver of the truck pulled into a makeshift parking area and Cade stopped alongside. The filthy-looking man with long, stringy black hair got out and motioned for them to follow him into a recreational vehicle.

"You good?" Kelly whispered to Cade as they ascended stairs to the door.

"I'm just dandy." He bobbed the toothpick between his teeth up and down a couple of times.

"Let's do this thing, little brother."

"Right behind you, big brother."

The RV was bright and relatively clean, much nicer than anything Kelly had seen so far. The big room held a sofa and a couple of chairs, which sat in front of a TV screen that was at least sixty inches. He gave a low whistle. "That's mighty nice."

"Shoe-ee!" Cade whooped it up. "Bet they don't have anything that fancy in the big house, do they, brother?"

"Shut your face," Kelly grumbled.

Cade laughed and turned to the man who'd brought them in. "My brother, here, just got out of Huntsville. He's a little *sens-i-tive*." He drew the word out.

"Told you to shut it," Kelly snapped.

The man chuckled. "What'd you do?"

Kelly blinked innocently. "I didn't *do* anything. *They say* I robbed a liquor store and shot the owner. *I say* one less colored in the world is doin' everybody a favor. Too bad the coon lived." Kelly's gut churned. They'd rehearsed trash talk like this, but it still pained him to say it. Several of his best friends were black, including Gus, and it was the chief who'd helped him practice speaking the hateful comments. Gus said he'd heard enough of them in his day.

"Now that's no shit!" The fellow suddenly seemed to have more appreciation for Kelly, so their plan was working.

Hate breeds hate. Kelly'd known from the beginning that going undercover in a white supremacist group wouldn't be easy or pleasant. He could only hope it would be worth it.

He glanced around. The RV appeared to be empty. "I thought you were taking us to see Boyd Bennett?"

"He'll be here."

Cade spoke up. "I'm Cade Mason and this here's my brother Kelly. Who are you?"

"People call me Sparky." He smiled, flashing a silver capped front tooth. "Some say it's because of my sparkling smile. I like to say it's because I enjoy setting fires and blowing things up."

"Cool." Cade's eyes sparkled like he was in awe.

Kelly bit back a smile.

The door opened and a clean-cut blond haired man entered, dressed in khakis and a white button down shirt. He was much better groomed than the other two they'd encountered and Kelly knew he had to be someone higher up in this branch of the organization. "Hello." The man smiled at them.

"Boyd Bennett?" Kelly asked.

"As promised. And you're the Mason brothers that Jesse Crawford told me to expect."

Kelly extended his hand. "Kelly Mason. This is my brother Cade."

Boyd shook with each of them. "Jesse said you'd be joining us. He just never explained why."

Kelly lowered his voice. "Did he tell you I just got out of Huntsville?"

Boyd smiled. "He may have mentioned that."

"Yeah, well these are tough times, and I'm worried about Cade, here. Jobs that pay anything are scarce and seldom easy. He's been hanging around with, shall we say, an *unsavory* crowd. I told him, like I'm telling you—I catch wind that he's selling drugs again I'm gonna kick his ass to the west coast and back. A man's gotta have some pride."

Cade puffed his chest out indignantly. "Like robbing a liquor store makes you something special."

Kelly grabbed Cade by the collar and faced him down. "No, it makes me a thief. But I wasn't popping pills or shooting up that shit you were pumping into your veins. Every decision I made, right or wrong, I made with a clear head. I want you to be able to say the same. And mostly, I don't want you to end up inside, like me."

Boyd studied them for a moment before nodding. "Your brother is right, Cade. We each have to choose our own path, our own direction. Our organization here is sort of like a training camp. By that I mean we realize there are a lot of distractions for young men out there today. What we do is provide discipline and structure. We help kids focus on what's important in life."

"I'm not a kid," Cade growled.

"I can see that, and I didn't mean to imply that you were. I'm closer to your brother's age, and tend to call anyone younger than me 'kid'. No offense intended."

Kelly swatted Cade's shoulder. "Sometimes he acts like a kid. I think he'd do better with some discipline. Our daddy used to provide that until he got sent away. Mama did her best, but we were headstrong growing up. Structure at home was, at best, lacking."

Cade smirked. "If you call getting walloped with a belt structure, then hell yeah, we got that."

Boyd bobbed his head. "That was your mama's job. I'll tell you right now, lots of guys here share the same story. But I'm not talking about that kind of discipline. We run this place more like a military boot camp, with a simple directive. A man needs to learn how to follow before he can lead. He should be able to set his own needs aside for the good of the group. We build character and create men with integrity."

Kelly raised his eyebrows. "Sounds impressive."

Cade rolled his eyes. "Sounds like the army. Not my idea of fun."

Boyd's smile widened. "Can you shoot?"

"Shit, yeah."

"He's one hell of shot," Kelly agreed.

"We like to shoot. Shotguns, rifles, even some heavy-duty artillery. It's part of our training, and I assure you, most of our boys agree that it's fun."

"How can you get away with that?" Cade asked.

"This ranch is set on a nice big plot of land, and hunting is legal. So we hunt." Boyd grinned. "And shoot things. And blow things up."

"Sounds kinda fun," Cade conceded. "But I ain't interested in enlisting, sorry."

"There's no enlisting involved. Our numbers are growing and nobody's in a hurry to leave. If anyone wants to, the door is wide open. Tell you what, come in for the weekend and check things out. If you don't like what you see, and don't think it's appealing then you're free to go. Everyone here is always free to leave at any time. We aren't the army. We have more intelligence behind us than any government run agency can boast about."

"I'd believe that." Kelly looked at Cade. "What do you say? Want to stay for a night or two and check things out?"

Cade hesitated. "I dunno."

Boyd looked at Kelly. "Would you like to stay with him? Generally, the fellows here are in the eighteen to twenty-five range. You're welcome to stay for the weekend and make sure everything is to both of your liking before you leave your brother with us."

Kelly scratched his chin and tried to appear thoughtful. *Eighteen to twenty-five, my ass. Those missing kids are fifteen and sixteen.* "Maybe so."

"Let's walk around the grounds, let you meet some of the others. Come with me." He led them out of the RV and headed down a path toward where Kelly knew the outbuildings were.

A scruffy, dark-haired man walked a ways in front of them.

"Wade!" Boyd called. "Wait up."

Kelly and Cade exchanged glances. *Wade Clements?*

The man walked back to meet them. He was grungier than his mugshot, but it was definitely Clements. "Yeah Boyd?"

"Wade, this is Cade." He chuckled at the rhyme. "How funny is that? *Wade and Cade.* Cade's thinking about joining us, so I invited him and his brother to stay for the weekend."

"Okay." Wade didn't seem amused by the joke, and wasn't very impressed to meet them. "I was just heading down to feed the dogs."

"Take Cade with you. Let him get a look around."

"Come on." Clements motioned to Cade, and started walking.

Cade shrugged at Kelly and Boyd, and then followed along.

"See you at the main house in an hour. Wade can show you where to go."

Cade tossed a small wave but didn't look back.

"He'll be fine." Boyd turned around. "Let's go back and get my truck. We'll drive to the main house. It's a couple of miles in."

"I'm not worried about him. He's a grown-assed man after all. I'm just trying to keep him from fucking up his life completely. Those drugs he was messing with are bad news." Kelly glanced around as they walked. "It sure is nice out here."

Boyd's eyes twinkled. "You may decide you want to stick around indefinitely. We could use a good man with real-world experience. If you're comfortable here, you may just want to consider it."

"Well now, you see, I'm not in any hurry to end up back in Huntsville. I need to keep myself squeaky clean."

Boyd blinked. "I'm saddened that you think our organization *isn't* squeaky clean."

Kelly smiled. "Like you said, I've been around the barrel a few times. You've got some kind of militia group here. Jesse wouldn't say much but he knows me, and knows what causes I support. I'm a member of the Texas Brotherhood." He rolled up his sleeve and showed the gang tattoo.

"Nice." Boyd examined the artwork. "I like this one, too." He pointed to Kelly's swastika and raised his own sleeve to display a similar symbol on his arm. "And does this look familiar?" His other arm sported a similar Texas Brotherhood image.

"TB? Cool. Always good to meet a brother."

"Yes, and in this day and age we have to stick together. There are a lot of forces against us, Kelly. We need to unite and keep the undesirables at bay."

"I'll help if I can. I ain't quite decided what my next move is gonna be. Might be I can stick around for a while, see how it goes."

"That sounds good. Real good." Boyd gave him a smile and his gaze practically seared into Kelly.

Kelly looked away quickly. Pure evil dwelt in those eyes. Regardless of what the man said, or how pleasant and charming he might appear, these were *not* good people. The minute he and Cade had what they came for they were history, and he wouldn't let the screen door hit his ass on the way out.

* * *

Cade followed Wade Clements to a makeshift dog pen off to the side of the barrack-type buildings. He counted eight large black dogs, mostly pit bulls and mixed breeds. "Holy shit. Are they dangerous?"

Clements scoffed. "They ain't house pets. But we feed them, so they're okay with us. When we stop feeding them, that's when you gotta watch out." He pulled a bag of dry food from a cabinet and poured it into their bowls over the top of the pen.

The dogs nosed each other out to reach the food, scarfing it down quickly.

Cade watched with surprise. The animals were starving. He hadn't given them much for as many of them as there were. "Why would you stop feeding them?"

Clements picked up a garden hose and turned on the spigot. He sprayed water through the fence until the dishes were mostly filled. "Huh?" He looked at Cade.

"You said 'when you stop feeding them is when you gotta watch out'. Why would you stop feeding them?"

Shrugging, Clements dropped the hose and turned off the spigot. He moved to go back the way they'd come. "Boyd thinks their reactions are sharper when they're hungrier. He doesn't want us to feed them too much."

"That's wild." Cade didn't say what he was really thinking. *That's bullshit.* He set his jaw and followed the man to catch up.

"Lots of wild things around here. It's a great place to hang out."

"Oh, yeah? I haven't decided if I'm staying or not. You been here long?"

"I was born here. This is my family's ranch. My folks moved into town, and now my father leases the property to Boyd's company."

"Really? That's cool. What's Boyd's company? I don't get what he does here."

Clements shot him a dirty look. "That's enough questions for now. Boyd will tell you what he thinks you should know."

"Whatever, man. He just made the offer for me to stay here, and I'm trying to decide what that means. If this is a pig ranch, am I gonna be slopping pigs all damn day? Is it a horse ranch? I wouldn't mind riding horses. Just wondering what I'll have to do if I stick around."

"Do you see any damn pigs or horses? Like I told you, Boyd will clue you in when he's good and ready. Now keep walking. It's another mile to the house."

"Great," Cade said dully. The conversation apparently over, they walked.

He considered himself to be in good shape, but he wasn't used to walking miles at a time. When they reached the main house he was sweating, and ready for an ice cold drink of anything.

"Wait here." Clements pointed to some benches on a brick patio. "I'll tell Boyd we're back."

"Can I get something to drink?"

"Hose is over there." Clements pointed to another garden hose, coiled on the side of the house. He entered through a sliding glass door, closing it behind him.

Cade surveyed the hose. "Thanks," he muttered to himself. "But I think I'll pass."

A few minutes later Boyd appeared in the doorway. "Come on in, Cade! You look thirsty after that walk. How about a nice glass of lemonade?"

"That'd be great."

Boyd motioned him in. "Don't just stand there. You're letting all the air conditioning out." He smiled welcomingly, something Clements hadn't done even once. There seemed to be two faces to the Clements ranch. One for prospective residents, and another for the current crew. Cade made a mental note to discuss it with Kelly when he got the chance.

He liked to leave himself reminders on his smartphone, but they'd left their personal cells behind. They each carried a burner flip phone for emergencies, with a few numbers programmed into speed dial. The number one would reach Gus, two called his boss at the ATF, and dialing the memory number nine would bring the full force of the Fort Worth PD along with FBI and ATF raining down upon the Clements ranch. He hoped they wouldn't need to use that one, but it was of some comfort to know it was available.

He followed Boyd inside where Kelly sat in a comfortable-looking living room drinking lemonade. Boyd motioned for him to take a seat, and sat across from them. "So how was your tour? Did you see everything?"

"I didn't see any pigs or horses." He accepted a glass from a plump, mousy-haired woman, and he smiled at her. "Thank you."

She made no eye contact, just set down a plate of cookies on the coffee table then hurried out.

Clements stood off to the side, although there were other places to sit. Cade watched him for a moment. They man eyed the cookies but never reached out for one.

Boyd took a drink then set his glass down. "We don't have pigs or horses here."

"That's what Wade said, when I asked what kind of a ranch this is. The only animals I've seen is a pack of starving dogs."

The head man chuckled. "The dogs are fed twice a day. If they're starving then Wade must not be doing his job correctly. Wade, are you doing your job correctly?"

"Yes sir. Feeding them twice a day." He shot Cade an evil look.

Cade figured it was the fourth such glance in less than an hour. He looked at Boyd expectantly, still waiting for an explanation of the ranch's purpose.

Boyd turned to Kelly. "We'll eat at six, then I thought you'd enjoy the bonfire we're having tonight. Might even scare up some marshmallows for S'mores. I've got a room for you and Cade here in the main house tonight. We're not fancy, but I think you'll be comfortable."

"Sounds fine." Kelly glanced around. "Do many of the recruits sleep here in the house?"

"No, we've got bunkhouse accommodations for the men. Again, not fancy, but the mattresses are in good shape and no one complains. Breakfast is at six, but if you're not quite used to our timeframe you could eat closer to seven."

"Six will be fine. We don't need special treatment. We want to meet the other guys and see what everyone does here."

"Then no special treatment it is. Enjoy your refreshments, and when you're ready, Monica will show you to your room. Take it easy a while, and I'll see you back here for chow." Boyd rose and left, Clements on his heels.

Cade watched them go, then looked at Kelly. "Guess no one really knows what kind of a ranch this is."

Kelly raised his brows. "Or no one wants to say." He brushed one finger across his lips in a shushing motion.

Cade nodded. They didn't know if they were truly alone, or even if the room might be bugged.

Despite the remark about special treatment, Kelly and Cade were two of only about six people at the dinner table. Monica served a hearty stew and cornbread, while Boyd kept the conversation light and pleasant.

"The food here is good," Kelly commented after he'd cleaned his plate.

"Sure is." Cade glanced at Boyd. "Eats this good all the time?"

"I enjoy my food," the man agreed. "I wouldn't settle for anything less."

Cade pushed his plate from the edge of the table and bit back a smile. After listening to Boyd Bennett for a few hours he could already read between the lines. Boyd didn't say that *everyone* ate this good, just him. So he wasn't actually lying...but he wasn't truthful, either. Cade wondered if other potential recruits had been lured in by the promise of S'mores and comfortable mattresses. He also wondered just how far from the truth those things were. Judging by the looks Wade Clements had given the cookies, he suspected the troops didn't eat so well once they'd signed on the dotted line.

He counted thirty people more or less when the bonfire lit up the night sky. By the glow of firelight it was hard to identify anyone, let alone Isaiah West, Stuart Falkner and Ben Lehman. He didn't see any black faces, so Isaiah was probably not there, as they'd suspected. The last photos of Stuart and Ben showed thin, tall young men with nearly shaved heads. That description fit most of the guys around the bonfire. On top of that, they were all dressed in camouflage pants and white T-shirts. Finding their two needles in this particular haystack might prove to be a challenge.

The S'mores consisted of one marshmallow, two squares of graham cracker and a small piece of chocolate. Cade didn't see anyone ask for seconds. He recalled high school bonfires where he and his friends would eat their hosts out of house and home. No one was *ever* shy about begging for more food. That was normal among teenagers. Nothing was normal with this crowd.

The get-together lasted about an hour, then the bonfire was extinguished and everyone went to bed. Kelly and Cade were shown back to the house, given fresh towels, and told good night.

Their bedroom was small, but had two twin beds and a comfortable chair. The bathroom across the hall housed a shower, but no tub. Cade didn't know how much the place had been remodeled, but it wasn't the usual layout for a family home.

"What do you think?" He asked Kelly when they were finally alone.

Kelly held a hand up. He began searching high and low and when he reached the lamp, came up with a small recording device. "Bugged," he mouthed.

Cade nodded. Glancing around, he came up with a pad and paper and began writing.

I feel like we're getting the royal treatment.

Kelly nodded and took the pencil. He replied,

Did you see the look on Clements face? Like he would have killed for a cookie this afternoon.

I saw that. Bennett is laying it on thick.

He told us that anyone can leave at any time.

Cade shook his head. *I don't believe that.*

Kelly stared at him.

Cade shrugged. *I know he said it. I just don't believe it. Like I don't believe the kids eat Monica's best cooking three meals a day. Today has been all about the show, for our benefit.*

Kelly nodded. *I didn't see Isaiah, but I can't swear to the other two.*

Agreed. They all look the same.

You ready to join their ranks? I thought tomorrow I'd ask Boyd if you could spend the night in the bunkhouse, get a real feel for the place.

I think it's the only way to find Stuart and Ben. If I can identify them, we'll make our excuses and head out on Sunday morning.

Best case scenario. Why do I feel like we won't get that lucky?

Cade grinned. *Because Karma is a bitch and you and I are two ornery sons of bitches?*

Kelly ran a hand through his hair, and jotted one last line. *There is that.*

He took the pad of paper and quietly removed the top sheet, then tore it into tiny bits.

Cade held out his hand. "Allow me." He scooped up the paper bits and walked across the hall, where he deposited them into the toilet then flushed the evidence away.

Chapter Thirteen

Cade flopped onto the cot he'd been assigned in the bunkhouse. They were standard military issue, but Boyd had been right. The mattresses and pillows were decent, and sleeping wouldn't be hard after the full and tiring day.

There'd been a few chores in the morning, then they'd spent several hours on an obstacle course made of pallets and tires. Racing on the course had brought the first signs of laughter and fun to the group that he'd seen. The guys seemed to take it seriously, and the kid who'd come out as the winner was especially pleased. Clements said he'd get a special reward, but hadn't disclosed anything else. Cade figured extra dessert might be a welcome reward in this place.

After a simple but filling lunch of ham and cheese sandwiches and vegetable sticks, they went to a firing range where they shot at cans and bottles for the next few hours. They ended the day with a few more chores, and grilled hamburgers and hot dogs for dinner.

It hadn't been an unpleasant day, but Cade couldn't shake the feeling that it still wasn't normal. Possibly the weekends were special, or activities had been modified to impress the guests. Either way, he wondered what a regular day would bring on the Clements' ranch. He really didn't want to stick around long enough to find out, but none of the boys had been friendly enough for him to strike up any conversations. They mainly kept to themselves in small groups.

After they'd eaten, he approached a group of three, pushing each other on a tire swing hung from a tree branch. "How's it going?"

"Okay," one of them replied, warily. "You the new guy?"

"Maybe. Haven't decided yet."

"You get to choose if you go or stay?" one of them asked Cade, his voice tinged with surprise.

"Well, sure. Boyd said it's cool either way. He said all of you are free to come and go as you please."

The three glanced at each other and laughed.

"That ain't true?" Cade watched their faces.

They stopped laughing and gave what appeared to be warning glances at one another.

"Whatever, man."

Cade sighed. "You know, I really would like to talk to some of you before I make a decision. It seems pretty cool here, but I just don't know."

"Appearances can be deceiving," one of them said.

"Ben!" another one snapped.

Cade perked up. *Ben.* "Your name Ben? I'm Cade Mason." He held out a hand to shake.

The boy glanced at him suspiciously before shaking his hand. "Ben Lehman. That there's Ronnie, and he's Steve."

"Good to meet you. So ya'll are pretty happy here? I mean, my brother wants to dump me off at this place, but I still don't know."

"Happy?" Ben looked at Ronnie and Steve. "Yeah, we're happy." His tone implied anything but. "We gotta go now. Curfew at dusk, have to be in the bunkhouse."

"Any of you know a guy named Stuart? One of my friends thought he might be here."

"I dunno." Ben turned to walk off.

Ronnie said, "Stewie's full name is Stuart, I think."

Steve elbowed him in the ribcage. "Shut up!" The boys wandered off after Ben.

Cade smiled. *Yes.* One down, one to go. *Now to find Stewie and make sure it's Stuart Falkner.* He might be home and calling Brandi the make-up artist for a second date before the weekend was up after all.

* * *

Kelly relaxed in the living room of the main house. He hadn't seen Boyd, but for a few minutes all day. The man had left him to his own accord. He'd nosed around when he could be sure Monica wasn't watching. There didn't seem to be any other household help.

There were no documents or papers of any kind lying around. One locked file cabinet sat in what appeared to be a neat and tidy office. He hadn't the time or the opportunity to try and get into it.

He'd seen Cade a couple of times. The recruits kept busy most of the day. He'd be interested to touch base with him and see what he'd learned, if anything, about the missing boys.

He felt guilty sleeping in the cool, comfortable house when Cade was practically camping out in the bunkhouse. *It's only a night or two.* Hopefully, it wouldn't take longer than that. It was just his second night away from home but he already missed Gillian and was ready to get back to her.

The house was dark and quiet. He strolled from room to room out of boredom. It wasn't even dark, but all activity had ceased. Kelly thought about taking a walk but considering how well armed the guards were, he didn't want to stumble into an area he shouldn't once the sun had gone down. *I'll leave the outside exploration to Cade. Maybe I can search the house again.* There had to be something useful there.

Entering the master bedroom for the first time, Kelly decided against turning on a light and instead used the pocket flashlight he carried with him. He knew the room to be Boyd's, and wondered how long he had to snoop before the man reappeared. Shining the light on the dresser, he peered at a few pieces of masculine jewelry. Silver cufflinks, an onyx ring, and a chain with a cross hanging from it. Nothing too expensive or ornate.

The click of a gun being cocked echoed in his ear.

"Looking for something?"

* * *

Cade slipped away from the group to do some exploring on his own. If he got caught now he could just say he'd taken a wrong turn and gotten lost. It'd be much harder to explain if he snuck out after the dusk-imposed curfew.

No one seemed to notice his leaving, or care if they did. He followed a dirt trail past several outbuildings, pausing to peer in each one as he passed. He hadn't found the exact building he'd stumbled upon the day he and Gus had come calling, so he continued looking to make sure the guns were still there.

Approaching the dog pens, he started to turn back in case the animals would bark when they spotted him. He saw two boys kicking rocks into a nearby gulch, so he got closer to hear what they were saying.

"You're damn lucky, Stewie. Winning on the obstacle course is going to give you one hell of an advantage in the hunt tomorrow."

Stewie! *How to find out if the kid was Stuart Falkner?* He listened again.

"You think? They haven't said what my reward would be."

"It has to be that."

"I don't know." Stewie picked up a rock and tossed it gently in the air then caught it again.

"I do." The other boy took the rock from Stewie's hand and pelted it at a nearby shed. "This hunt is going to be majorly rad."

"I don't like hunting the dogs. I wish they wouldn't make us do that."

"They're stupid animals. Who cares about them? But tomorrow ain't gonna be no dog. Tomorrow we're hunting coon." He approached the shed he'd just hit with the rock and peered between two boards. "Boo!" he yelled through the crack, then roared with laughter as the boys ran off.

Cade's gut lurched. *Hunting dogs?* Were these boys brainwashed into thinking that was okay? He took a step toward the shed. Had they caught another wild animal to prey upon? He remembered that first day, when he'd seen one of them shooting at a squirrel.

He glanced inside, wondering if they'd caged a raccoon or just let him run free in the shed. The two eyes peering back at him did not belong to a raccoon. Best he could tell, under the dirt and grime, they belonged to Isaiah West.

* * *

Kelly winced as Boyd Bennett jerked his arms behind his back and clicked metal handcuffs on his wrists.

Beads of sweat forming on his brow, Boyd faced Kelly and scowled. "I should have known you were trouble from the minute you waltzed in here. I called a friend of mine who works in the office at Huntsville Prison. She couldn't find any record of a Kelly Mason ever having been there."

"You're right. I shouldn't have lied to you. My name isn't Mason. My real name is Kelly Waters. That's the name my record is under. I changed it when I got out. Aiming for a fresh start and all."

"And if I call my friend, she'll find Kelly Waters in the prison computer?"

"I was there. Unit twenty-four, cellblock D, cell nine." Kelly's mind raced as he dug himself deeper and deeper. He needed to

235

stall long enough to get to his cell phone and call in the Calvary. It was going to be tricky given his present situation, and Boyd's 44 revolver.

"That explains it then. I should let you go." Boyd moved behind him and reached for Kelly's hands.

Before Kelly knew what was happening, the man lifted his bound arms and kicked him forcefully in the small of his back. He lurched forward and fell to the floor.

"Just kidding." Boyd stood over him with one boot against Kelly's neck. "You already admitted that you lied to me. Fool me once, shame on you. Fool me twice—well, no one has ever lived long enough to fool me twice."

The front door opened and Kelly glanced sideways to see Cade being forced in by Wade Clements. His hands were behind his back but Kelly couldn't tell if he was cuffed or not.

"Boss, we got problems." Clements words came out in a rush.

"Oh for fuck's sake, what did this one do?"

"Caught him snooping around by the coon shed. Had his phone out."

Boyd scrambled away from Kelly over to Cade. "Where's the phone?"

Clements pulled it from his pocket and offered it up.

He snatched the phone then backhanded Cade, who stumbled to the floor.

His hands aren't cuffed. Kelly's mind raced.

Boyd turned to Clements and smacked him in similar way. "I told you to keep an eye on him."

"I did! He snuck off when I went to feed the dogs is all."

Boyd snapped open the phone and his fingers flew over the keys. He looked at Cade. "Who did you call?"

Cade adjusted his jaw with one hand. "No one."

Boyd's response was to kick Cade in the gut. "I'll ask again, who did you call?"

The low wail of sirens could be heard in the distance.

"Well, I guess that answers *that* question."

"You have the recruits hunt the *dogs*?" Cade gazed up at him defiantly.

Kelly could see Boyd's face getting red, and tried to take his attention away from Cade. "That's sick, man," he muttered.

Cade leaned up on one elbow. "Wait 'til you hear what else they hunt. Or should I say 'who'." He glanced at Kelly. "I found Isaiah West. He's the 'coon' they were planning to hunt tomorrow."

Boyd kicked Cade in the stomach again but this time Cade grabbed his boot and brought the man to his back. Cade scrambled to get Boyd's gun, but Clements beat him to it, pointing the revolver at Cade. "Enough!"

Cade froze.

Boyd climbed to his feet. "These two are history." He took his gun back and looked at Clements. "Take this one to the shed and lock him up with the kid. We'll have two pests to hunt tomorrow."

Cade glared at him. "I told the police about Isaiah. They'll be looking for him."

Pacing back and forth, Boyd came up with a new plan. "Poor kid wandered in here after dark. We offered him food and shelter until tomorrow, when someone was going to drive him home." He smiled. "They have no reason not to believe my story. Especially when neither of you will ever be seen again."

He turned to Clements. "Gag him, and make sure you tie him up tight. Stick him in that farthest shed out back. No one will look there in the dark. Then get the coon out and clean him up. We'll offer him over and that should satisfy the law."

"What about that one?" Clements motioned to Kelly.

"Oh, he's mine. I'm not sure who he is, but I suspect he's some kind of law. I'm going to take my time with that one. When I'm finished, he'll regret the day he came to Clements' ranch."

"We're already regretting it," Cade spouted. "Better tie me up now, Wade.

Between you and me, alone out there in the dark, I'm liable to get the jump on you if you don't."

Kelly watched with disbelief. *Hope he has a plan.*

Boyd rubbed his chin with his gun hand. "He's right. There's some rope and another gun in my closet. Go get them."

Clements hurried out.

Before Boyd could turn around, Cade jumped him and wrestled the gun from his hand.

Boyd reached for it and Cade shot him in the arm, then the knee.

He fell to the floor.

"Watch out!" Kelly called as Clements reappeared in the doorway, brandishing the rope and another revolver.

Cade spun around and shot him in the stomach.

Clements dropped.

Cade retrieved the gun and looked at him.

"You shot me!" Clements clutched his waist in disbelief.

"It's just a gut shot. You'll live. I hear tell they have really good hospitals in prison."

He glanced at Boyd as he passed him.

The man was nursing his own, non-life threatening injuries. "Thought you were supposed to be a good shot?"

Cade smiled. "Mister Bennett, if I'd have wanted to kill you, you'd be dead by now." He pulled his keys from his pocket and unlocked Kelly's cuffs, then offered a hand to pull him up.

Kelly got to his feet, and accepted the gun Cade handed him. "Thanks for saving my bacon."

"Thank you for the warning shout." Cade smiled again. "Seems we make a pretty good team."

Still trying to process the quick succession of events, Kelly shook his head to clear it. "Seems we do. You wanna get back on the horn and advise the Calvary that we need a couple of ambulances? Tell them to see to Isaiah West first. We got these two."

Cade grinned. "I surely will."

Chapter Fourteen

"Damn girl, you're like a *Cat on a Hot Tin Roof*." Cam switched his bar towel and just caught the cheek of his wife's bum with the edge. She'd been darting from the kitchen, back to the bar and out to the picnic tables and back again, scrubbing and polishing and shining everything in sight.

"Hell, it's just Kelly and Gillian and a couple of their cop buddies."

"Not to mention the County Sheriff, a representative from ATF and his bosses and probably an FBI agent or two thrown in for good measure. You think I want them coming in here and wiping down the seats before they feel like they can set their shiny butts on them?"

Cam shook his head. "If you get this place any cleaner all my regulars goin' to be heading on over to the Bait Shack just to get some proper beer drinkin' atmosphere. Like I said *Cat*."

"I'll give you a hot *Cat*, Mr. Smarty pants." Stella raised her dusting cloth and her husband dashed to the end of the bar and ducked for safety.

"Coward." She climbed onto a stool in front of him then reached across the bar to pull him back into her arms and plant a big smooch on his lips.

"Don't get ideas." She giggled when her husband responded by reaching across the bar and scooping all one hundred fifteen pounds of her off her barstool and onto the top of the bar.

"Who me?" Cam had both hands under her shirt and was working his way south when the door to the bar opened.

Stella jumped out of his arms, straightened her shirt and turned to face the door.

"Ah ha, caught you didn't I?" Gillian stood in the doorway with laughter blooming all over her face.

Stella blushed and Cam escaped out to the patio, mumbling something about checking his smoker.

"You two are so cute." Gillian joined Stella at the bar. "So what do you need me to do?"

"Not a thing. Did you see the notice out front?"

"Yes. *Closed for a Private Function.* How'd you manage to convince Frank and Doug they weren't included?"

"I left that part up to Cam. I don't know what he told them but I was back in the kitchen when I heard them head for the door. Of course Frank was mumbling something about public facilities being commandeered for private stuff. You'd think this was an offshoot of the Social

Security office and he was being denied his constitutional rights.”

“You gotta love them. I suppose they headed on down to the Bait Shack.”

“You nailed it. Cam told me I had it smelling too clean in here anyhow, that’s what we were bickering about when you crashed the party.”

“From what I could see through the peek in the door it didn’t exactly look like what comes to my mind when I hear a couple ‘bickering’.”

“Ha ha! Just for that you can help me wrap onions for the smoker. I need to run to the house to get them out of the refrigerator. We ran out of room in this one.”

Stella pointed towards the gleaming stainless steel kitchen that Cam had managed to include when he’d remodeled the bar after his parents retired. The Hideaway had become famous for its weekend barbecues. For the first couple of years things had been tight for Cam, but then a bunch of stock he’d bought because he believed in a kid named Mark Zuckerberg split and re-split and share prices went through the roof. Cam sold his shares, and the re-invested windfall meant he’d never have to work another day in his life.

Stella, sighed. She didn’t really want to be a bar maid, but Cam loved the Hideaway. After the summer was over she’d have to make a decision about what in hell she really wanted to do with her life. Cam's bar kept him happy, and she loved that, but she had to find something more for herself.

"Earth to Stella."

"Sorry, got caught up in daydreaming. Okay. Let's get to work before Cam comes in here and cracks the whip.

Gillian laughed. "As if. You and Cam are the cutest couple I've ever met. Talk about a match made in heaven."

Stella's smile lit up her face. "Thanks Gill. I love that man so much. I never imagined that kind of love would happen to someone like me, but I thank my lucky stars every day I'm breathing that I met all of you out here at Indian Creek. Best days of my life, and best friends."

"You'll have me crying." Gillian hugged her friend. "Now go get the onions."

While she waited for Stella, Gillian wandered around the big main room of the bar. Stepping inside the Hideaway was like taking a trip down memory lane. The décor—a tribute to the owner's passion for country music and country living—was a potpourri of tools and implements from the turn of the century. Cam proudly displayed his collection of antique beer wagons in a glass case behind the bar. His *piece-de-resistance* being a cherished replica of the Budweiser Clydesdales rigged out in full harness. Even the ceiling bore witness to Cam's passion. Glossy black and white photos of Hank Williams, Patsy Cline, Faron Young, and a whole slew of long-dead country favorites smiled down on the patrons.

"Sorry I took so long." Stella came through the double doors that led out onto the patio holding a grocery bag in each hand. "It's nice and warm outside now. We might as well leave these doors open." She set the bags down while she snapped the fasteners on each side that held the heavy doors back.

"Here, let me help you." Gillian joined Stella at the door. "It smells wonderful." She breathed in the mingled aromas of brisket, barbecued pork and spicy Texas chili and suddenly clutched her stomach. "Whew. I don't know what's the matter with me this past week." She turned to Stella. "Every time I smell food, no matter how delicious, my stomach turn into a roller coaster."

Stella had been puzzled watching Gillian. Now, when her friend reached for one of the bags, Stella put out a hand and stopped her. "I'll get these. You go sit down for a minute. You're pale as a ghost. Have you been sick?"

Gillian shook her head. "No. I'm fit as a fiddle. This food nonsense started a couple weeks after we got back from our trip. It doesn't make any sense. I'm fine, I go out in the morning, do all my chores feeling great, come back into the house, go to fix breakfast and I'm suddenly sick as a dog. It's embarrassing, if you want the truth. Poor Kelly has been making most of our meals since we got home."

"Hang on." Stella took the bags of onions into the kitchen, set them down on the counter and hurried back out to Gillian. "Okay, you come sit down over here." She took Gillian's arm and led her over to one of the booths. "Now stay here. I'll be right back."

Gillian, still a bit too shaky to protest, leaned her head back on the soft leather of the booth.

"Cam." Stella called out to her husband.

"What's up?" He strode through the open doors with a barbecue fork in his hand.

"I need you to take care of the onions. Gillian's not feeling too good. I'm going to run her back to the house and have her lay down for a bit." Stella leaned in toward Cam and whispered something in his ear.

"Oh!" His eyes lit up. "You really think so?"

"Shhh. Why don't you give Leroy a call, have him come over and help you get the rest of the food ready, I'll stay back at the house with Gillian until everyone gets here."

"Sure, no problem. You go take care of her." Cam walked towards the bar phone with the biggest grin on his face Stella had ever seen, she watched him as he dialed and spoke into the phone.

"Okay my love," he called back to Stella. "You ladies are officially released from kitchen duty. The Cavalry in the persons of Leroy and Margaret are on their way over."

"I don't know what's gotten into me," Gillian told Stella after losing her lunch in the bathroom and staggering back to the kitchen. "I wish I could be more help, but apparently I've caught something that just isn't going away. I hope you don't mind but I really need to go home."

"Nonsense. You're not going home. I've got the guest room all made up for you. All you need is a couple of hours sleep and you'll be right as new. Now go on in there and take a nap while I go out and supervise the cooking crew. You know you want to be here when Kelly and his crew show up, so I don't want to hear another word about going home."

"You don't think I might be contagious?"

Stella laughed. "I guarantee you there's no one coming whose going to catch what you've got. Now climb into that bed." Stella had been leading her down the hall as they talked and inside the bedroom with the blinds lowered and the comfy white and yellow duvet on the bed, Gillian sank into the feathery soft mattress and didn't protest when Stella removed her shoes.

"I'll be back in an hour or two. You get some sleep."

"I am tired. Maybe a nap will make me feel up to the barbecue. Don't take it personally though, if I can't eat anything."

Stella smiled and left the room. Back at the Hideaway she stopped for a word with Cam. Said hi to Leroy and Margaret and thanked them for taking her place, then headed for the Lake Country Market.

It took her an hour, picking up a few things for Cam as well as what she hoped would be a welcome surprise for Gillian.

"I think that's the fastest shopping trip you've ever made," Cam commented when she dropped off the condiments he'd wanted. "You going to do it now?"

"That's the plan. I'll let you know how it goes."

Cam grinned. "Hot dog. Wait'll Kelly gets here."

"You just keep quiet. This is husband and wife stuff, not best buddies swapping yarns."

Cam lifted his eyebrows and smirked. "I know, but hurry it up will you."

Stella shook her head and headed back to the house. Grabbing the package out of her purse, she knocked gently on the bedroom door.

"Come in. I'm awake," Gillian responded.

Stella opened the door, walked over to the bed and sat down beside her friend. "How do you feel?"

"Better actually. That's what so strange about this I'll feel just fine and then all of a sudden I'm in the bathroom heaving my breakfast."

"I know." Stella brushed Gillian's hair back and looked into her eyes. "I've got something for you. Now don't get upset, just take this, go into the bathroom and bring it back out when you're done."

Gillian looked at the package, read the label, and sat straight up in the bed. "No."

Stella laughed. "I think, yes. Listen, if I'm wrong, no harm done, but if I'm right it'll explain everything you've been going through."

Five minutes later the two of them sat side-by-side on the bed staring at the big blue plus sign in the window of the Clear Blue monitor.

"Oh, my God." Gillian kept saying over and over again.

"Hey. You and Kelly are going to be wonderful parents."

Gillian shook her head. "But I just never thought. I've never told you, but I was injured in a jumping competition when I was thirteen. I broke my pelvis and the doctors told me at the time that I'd probably never have children. How can this be?"

"Just goes to show, doctors don't always know what they're talking about."

Gillian, still with a dazed expression on her face, looked up at Stella. "I need to tell Kelly. I told him we wouldn't be able to have children. What's he going to think now?"

"If I know Kelly, and next to you I think I probably know him better than anyone around here, except maybe Gus. He's going to be such a button popping, testosterone strutting proud papa to be that you'll be sneaking out here just to get a break."

Gillian smiled and Stella reached out and hugged her friend. "Now don't you worry, I've got this all figured out. You don't want to be telling Kelly the news while the whole gang is sitting around out there. I'm going to run over to the bar right now and tell him you're not feeling well and you need him back at the house."

"What if he isn't here yet?"

"I heard a few vehicles pull up while you were in the bathroom. One of them sounded just like Old Blue, so he's probably jawing with Cam. You go freshen up and I'll send him back to you."

Gillian had kind of a far-away look in her eyes when she smiled at Stella and reached for her hand. "Thanks, friend."

"My pleasure. Dibbs on Godmother, okay?"

"As if I'd even consider anyone else."

Back at the Hideaway, Jackie and the Texas Troubadours were out on the patio tuning up their instruments, and Leroy and

Margaret had outdone themselves with all the food and preparations.

"You put on a spread like this and you'll never get these ATF boys out of your hair." Kelly clapped Cam on the shoulder and took a big sniff of the aromas floating in from the patio.

"Hey, nothing but the best. Don't want them city boys thinking were a bunch of hicks that don't know how to do it up right." Cam nodded across the room to where Cade was busy chatting up the cute blonde behind the bar. "That one of them there?"

"Yep, that's Cade. I see you got yourself a new bartender."

"Stella pretty much laid the law down. She didn't mind filling in when Darlene retired, but she made it clear bartending wasn't on her resume and she hadn't ever intended to see it there."

"Sounds like Stella. Didn't take Cade long to spot that one." Kelly chuckled. "The boy's a hound dog when it comes to the scent of a pretty young women."

"Is this a private conflab or can anyone join in?" Stella put an arm around each of their shoulders and leaned in between them.

"Hi there Stella, I was just telling Cam he'd never get rid of the ATF boys if he fed them like it smells like he's going to. Say, where's my wife?"

"Oh, she's over at the house. She asked me to send you back when you came along.

She had a bit of an upset stomach earlier and I took her back there so she could rest before the party."

"Again?" Kelly shook his head. "That's not at all like Gillian. She never gets sick, but lately she can't seem to keep anything down. I wanted her to go to the doctor when we got back from Vegas, but you know how she is, that girl figures she's invincible."

"I think she's okay now. Why don't you go on over there and join her?" Stella smiled and steered Kelly towards the back patio.

* * *

I don't care what she says this time. Kelly set his mouth in a firm line as he jogged across the back lawn and stopped to open the small gate leading from the Hideaway to Stella and Cam's place. *She's going to the doctor tomorrow if I have to carry her there.*

Kelly walked in the back door of the house and called out to his wife. "Hey Gill, are you in here?"

"I'm back here." Her soft voice came from the back and Kelly started toward the sound.

"Are you okay?" He walked into the bedroom and looked down at his wife, lying on the bed with her hair spread around her face and her head resting on Stella's satin pillow. "Do you need me to take you to the doctor?"

"Kelly, come over here." Gillian patted the bed. "I think you need to sit down before I give you my news."

Kelly sat on the side of the bed and reached for her hand. "Listen Gill, you're scaring me. What's going on?"

"We're going to have a baby."

He looked at her with a completely blank expression on his face. "What?"

"You heard me, we're going to have a baby."

"Oh my God, oh my God. Gilly are you sure? I thought you couldn't have kids?"

"Well, I'm 99.9% sure according to the Clear Blue Plus test Stella just gave me, and considering I have all the signs of pregnancy, I'd say that makes it pretty darn certain."

Kelly leaned down, wrapped his arms around her and pulled her close to his chest.

After several moments, Gillian lifted her head and looked up into his face. "Kelly, you're crying."

"Nope. Just hot in here. Oh Gilly, I can't begin to tell you how much I've wanted a child. It's something that I figured was never in the cards for me. I love you with all my heart, and when you said you couldn't have kids, I just decided the man upstairs didn't need my help increasing the surplus population."

Gillian burst out laughing at Kelly's reference to the line from the old Scrooge classic they watched together every Christmas Eve. "Guess he changed his mind. Now let's get out of this bedroom and go join the festivities."

Strolling hand in hand across the grass and back to the patio Kelly stopped and looked down at his wife. "I love you."

"And I love you."

"Do you care if I tell Cam? I won't say anything to the rest of them, we probably better wait until you see the doctor, but Cam, I gotta tell him."

"Of course you can, although if I know my Stella, you're probably going to be second in line."

"Damn that woman."

The patio was bathed in light from the strings of bulbs strung around the railings and up through the branches of giant pecan trees that hung, heavy with nuts, over the patio. Along the far side of the platform, Cam was pulling racks out of a giant sized smoker and as he set the platters of meat on the food-laden table beside the smoker, mouth-watering aromas scented the air.

Kelly escorted Gillian inside to where Stella was mixing cocktails.

"I'm going to hang in here with Stella while you go out there and jaw with all the lawmen." Gillian hopped up on a barstool and gave Kelly a kiss on the cheek.

"You need me, you yell." Kelly turned to look at Stella behind the bar. "You already tell the big guy?"

Stella's guilty smile answered the question.

Kelly shrugged. "Okay, big mouth. You look after my little momma while I go see to the guys." He headed outside to where Gus and two of his deputies, along with Cade and the ATF agents who'd stayed behind were set up at a long table with two ice-filled pails of longnecks and an assortment of cocktails served by Stella's young trainee.

"Hey Cam," Kelly called out to where his friend had been setting out trays of sliced brisket, sauced up ribs, pulled pork, quartered chickens, and a side pan of smoked onions.

"I see you got your group out here okay." Cam strolled over to the table. "I hope ya'll's hungry." He smiled at the men around the table. "Food's on whenever you're ready to grab your plates."

"Now that's an invitation I never turn down." Gus turned to Cade who had parked himself on the bench beside the big detective. "Cam, this here is Cade Wyatt." Gus got up from his seat, while Cade shook hands with Cam and introduced him to the rest of the ATF team.

"Ya'll can sit there getting acquainted as long as you like," Gus said over his shoulder as he headed for the heavily laden table.

"Wow, look at all that food." Cade had wasted no time joining Gus and both of them grabbed plates and started loading up from dishes of baked beans, potato salad, stuffed jalapenos and chunky slabs of garlic toast along with man-sized portions of beef, pork, chicken and onions.

After filling their plates, everyone took seats at the table. Kelly put a few things on a plate for Gillian. She sat next to him and Stella next to her, and they ate while the men talked.

"I thought the food at the Clements' Ranch was good," Cade joked. He leaned in to the bartender, Lily, whom he'd convinced to fix a plate and grab a seat next to him. "It was an assignment we just finished up. Top secret government stuff."

"Wow." She batted her eyelashes at him in awe.

Kelly grinned and shook his head. "That woman Monica was a fine cook. But it was easy to tell the boys didn't eat that way all the time. I'm not sure what they were fed, or how much."

Gus wiped his mouth with a napkin. "You got the prospective recruit treatment?"

"Oh yeah. Cookies, lemonade, the works." Cade shook his head. "That's what first tipped me off. Seeing the look on Wade Clements' face when we got cookies. He looked like a starved pup."

"That's sad, really," Gillian offered.

Kelly nodded. "What's sad is that they treated the boys and the dogs about the same."

"Unless you were a dark-skinned boy," Cade interjected. "Then you were treated worse."

Gus cleared his throat. "Yeah, well, Boyd Bennett is going behind bars for a good long time after everything that was confiscated from that place. And Wade Clements will have some charges added to his probation violation so he's going away, too. Funny thing, he didn't seem all that upset about it."

Cade shrugged. "Maybe prison is preferable to the ranch after all."

Stella added, "I hope they cleared that place out. We don't need some other group of militant crazies trying to move in and take over."

"Oh, no." Gus shook his head. "When Wade's daddy found out what had been going on out there on his leased property, he went through it with a bulldozer. The underage kids were all released to their parents, including Ben and Stuart who were happy to go home at that point."

"What about that little Isaiah?" Gillian asked.

"He was hospitalized as a precaution," Kelly replied. "He's going to need some therapy, but he's got a loving family. They lost one son to war and they got no intention of losing another. They were holding on pretty tight to each other, last time I saw them.”

“Good.” She reached for his hand and squeezed.

Kelly gazed at her, love swelling in his heart. His cell phone jangled and he sighed. “Kinda makes me long for the days when our phones stayed at home on the wall.” He smiled at her then answered the call. “Kelly McWinter.”

“Kelly, how are you? It’s Mark Fischer.”

He rose from the table and whispered, “Excuse me,” to his wife and friends. He stepped away for privacy before replying. “Mark, hey there. Are you back from Russia?”

“No, I’m not. I have another couple of months here. I hate being away from Marcy but if I don’t get this job done now I’ll have to do it later. And I know I won’t want to come back here when she’s close to delivery, or after the baby is born.”

From a distance, Kelly watched Gillian chat with Stella. “I understand how you feel.”

“But listen, we have a problem. Lucas Spadina’s been spotted in Nashville. He hasn’t been seen around the house, but even the same state is too close for me.”

Rubbing his temple, Kelly sighed again. “I’m sorry to hear that, Mark, but didn’t you hire a round the clock surveillance team for Marcy and her family?”

"The security service we engaged is good, no doubt about it. But they aren't family like you are Kelly. Marcy feels close to you and Gillian. She'd be much more comfortable with you there, and in her condition, I want her as calm and relaxed as possible. I can send the jet for you tonight. How soon can you two be ready?"

Kelly's gut churned. He had a wife who also needed to stay as calm and relaxed as possible, but he couldn't tell anyone that yet. No way in hell was he taking Gillian to Tennessee. He wasn't sure he wanted to go himself. Things were different now. "Mark, let me think about it. I've got cases here I need to work on, and I'm honestly not sure I can get away right now."

"We don't trust anyone as much as we trust you, Kelly."

"I hear you."

"I'm just sayin'."

"I'll take it under advisement."

"Does this mean you're not coming tonight?"

"I'll call you tomorrow, buddy." He ended the call and took a few deep breaths to calm down. He sure didn't like the position Mark had put him in. There was no way he was leaving Gillian alone now but he hated the idea of disappointing Marcy and her family. All the worry bubbled around in his gut until he no longer had an appetite.

Rejoining everyone at the table, he sat and pushed his fork around the plate.

"Everything okay?" Gillian smiled at him.

He smiled back. "Couldn't be better."

* * *

Kelly's phone woke him at six-thirty the next morning. He vaguely heard the music but didn't rush to answer it. He was comfortable where he was, wrapped around his wife with his face buried in her hair. The stupid thing was gonna have to ring more than once to get his attention.

Twenty minutes later Gillian was begging him to answer it.

"Need sleep," he muttered into her hair.

"So do I, sugar. Either turn the fool thing off or quiet the ringtone."

Grumbling at having to move, he grabbed the cell and saw the missed calls were from Gus. "Gus. Damn it!"

"Ignore him," she advised.

He could ignore many calls, but Gus and his wife were two people that he felt obliged to answer. He didn't feel obliged to be that nice at this hour, though, and answered, "Do you realize what time it is?"

"Damn it, Kelly, you know I wouldn't call this early if it wasn't important. Apparently there was an incident at Marcy Fischer's house in Nashville last night."

Kelly froze. "What kind of incident?"

"That stalker fella broke in and was killed by the security people on duty."

"Is Marcy okay?"

"She's fine. I guess she wasn't even home. It's a sad thing, but don't think for a minute anyone's unhappy that the guy is out of the picture."

Kelly's breathing slowly returned to normal. "God, Gus, if Mark had gotten his way, Gill and I would have been there last night. He wanted to send the jet for us."

"You wouldn't have taken her, would you? In her condition?"

Kelly blinked. "What are you talking about?"

"Son, I've seen my wife and daughters have morning sickness that lasted all damn day for up to three months. Tell Gilly that Betty has some home remedies that'll make her feel better in no time."

He smiled. "I'll pass that along. Thanks, man."

"Talk to you later."

Kelly tossed his phone on the nightstand and snuggled back into position.

Gillian ran a hand through his hair. "What did he want?"

He opened one eye and looked at her. "I guess we're done sleeping?"

"I asked a simple question, sugar."

"With a not-so-simple answer. Lucas Spadina was shot and killed at Marcy's house in Nashville last night."

She lifted an eyebrow. "Oh. So exactly why were you and I almost there?"

"Mark called when we were at the Hideaway. He wanted us to come and watch out for Marcy. He told me Spadina had been spotted in Nashville, and in Marcy's delicate condition, he didn't want her under any stress."

She gave a lazy smile. "So to keep his pregnant wife from stress you're going to take your pregnant wife halfway across the country to look for a crazed stalker?"

"Nope. I had no such intention. This baby changes things, Gill. I'm not just taking care of you anymore, I'm taking care of you and our baby."

Marcy laughed and snuggled closer. "It's a tad early to be confining me to bedrest, but I agree, it's time to make some decisions about our life. As much as it pains me to say it, I won't be riding my horses until after the baby comes. I don't want to take any chances."

"Agreed. And I'll be choosier about the cases I accept. I'll be needing to stay closer to home."

"You do realize that's going to decrease our income. Not that we'll need to file for federal aid or anything, but a good share of your cases in the past have involved travel. I'm in favor of you cutting back, as long as you're aware of the cut in pay you'll be taking."

He scratched his head. "Maybe there's a way I can have my cake and eat it, too."

"You mind explaining that little ditty?"

"Later." He nuzzled her neck. "Right now I plan to make love to my pregnant wife. You got a problem with that?"

She ran a hand over his stubbled cheek and smiled. "Sugar, I've got no problems in the world."

Epilogue

Seven months later
Kelly and Gillian stood inside the old Barn that had served as the Indian Creek flea market for the past twenty years. After Kelly married and moved to the ranch with Gillian, the owner, Shorty Williams, had decided to shut the operation down. The barn and outbuildings had been sitting empty for over a year, and when Kelly came up with the idea of opening an agency the Indian Creek location popped into his head like it had been destined all along.

They'd had workmen on site for several month now converting two of the former flea market stalls into an office for Kelly, with the rest of the three-sided stalls ready for his new detectives as they came on board.

Kelly finished hanging the sign on his office door and stepped back to admire his handiwork. *McWinter Confidential.* "It's got a nice ring to it. What do you think?"

Gillian waddled up next to him, her pregnant belly leading the way. "I think it's amazing. I'm so happy Shorty made you a deal on the flea market property. He hasn't used it since he retired and the barn is perfect office space for you and your new team.”

Cade approached with a box of supplies from the back of his Jeep. “It is pretty cool out here. I never knew this place existed in Indian Creek. It’s a great location.”

Kelly smiled. “I’m happy to have someone living in my cabin again. I could never see fit to get rid of it, but I won’t need it anymore.”

Inside the barn-turned-office, Cade set the box down on his new desk. “I surely appreciate the rental, and the job. I’ve known for a while now that I needed a change from the ATF. My mama’s not well and the old man could use some help looking after her.”

“How long does it take you to drive from here to Denton?” Gillian asked.

“Forty, forty-five minutes in good traffic. That’s about perfect. I love my folks, you know, but I don’t want them *too* close.” Cade winked.

Kelly pondered that as he rubbed his chin. “How do you define *too* close, Cade? Is Brandi the make-up artist leaving an hour before Lily the bartender gets here *too* close?”

Cade grinned. “I’d say that’s just about perfect.”

“Yoo hoo!” Stella joined them in the office. “Hey, it’s really taking shape in here!”

Speaking of too close... Cade muttered *sotto voce.*

Stella ruffled his hair as she passed. "Aw, now, Weston, just because I don't let you walk all over my bartender, and I call you out when I think you're taking advantage of your lady friends, don't be a poor sport."

He shot her a look. "Don't call me that."

She gazed at him innocently. "What? A poor sport?"

"You know what I meant."

She picked up the framed PI license from the top of his box. "It says right here, Weston Cade Wyatt. I'm just calling you by your name."

He smiled through gritted teeth. "I've got a few names for you, too."

Laughing, Stella waved him off and stepped in front of Kelly. "Well, I couldn't tell you before now because I knew you wouldn't believe me, but it came in the mail today, so here I am."

He shook his head. "Once more, in English? I'd settle for something vaguely Texan."

She laughed. "Look what I did while y'all were traipsing across the country relaxing the past few months." She held up a certificate that looked strangely like Cade's.

Kelly blinked. "Oh, no."

"Oh, yes. I got my PI license! I figured you couldn't hire him without hiring me to keep that hooligan in check."

"Oh, no," Cade echoed.

Gillian clapped her hands. "Oh, yes! This is amazing! Stella can help out with the business stuff too, because she's a whiz at that kind of thing. Oh, Kelly, this is just perfect. Exactly what we needed to get our agency going."

He swallowed. With Gill on board, there was no way to bow out gracefully. He glanced at Cade. "Looks like we have a new team member."

Cade's smile was less than genuine. "Wonder if it's too late to get my old job at the ATF back?"

Kelly nudged him with his elbow. "We'll make it work. We could use someone to run the office."

"True."

Stella cocked her head. "I'm gonna do more than that. Just wait and see! You won't know—" Her phone rang and she paused to answer it. "McWinter Confidential, Stella speaking. Oh, hey, honey! No, I was just joking. This is still my number. What? What? Oh Marcy, congratulations!" She held the phone away from her ear. "Marcy just had her baby. Seven pounds, three ounces, twenty inches long."

"Well?" Gillian's eyes sparkled. She and Stella had been crazy with curiosity not knowing the baby's sex.

Stella grinned. "It's a girl. Loretta Lynn Fischer."

"Aww!" Gill clutched her chest. "Bless their little hearts. Tell Marcy I'm gonna call her real soon."

Kelly slid an arm around his wife's waist. "And tell her congrats from all of us."

"Will do." Stella returned to the call, and Cade proceeded to unpack his stuff.

Kelly pulled up a chair and sat so he faced Gill's belly. "Hey, son." He kissed the baby through her shirt. "I hope your mama doesn't have any grand ideas about naming you Blake Shelton McWinter."

Gill laughed and ran a hand through Kelly's hair. "Blake is a pretty cute name. We'd better start narrowing down our choices, you know."

He gazed up and kissed her stomach one more time. "I know, 'cause we're next!"

The End

Also from Books We Love
by Author Jude Pittman

Kelly McWinter PI series
Deadly Secrets
Deadly Betrayal
Deadly Consequences

Sisters of Prophecy Series
Katherine, Book 1
Bad Medicine – Novella

Canadian Historical Brides Series
Pillars of Avalon, Book 5
Katherine Pym and Jude Pittman
Canadian romantic suspense and mystery
author Jude Pittman is one-half of the
corporate team behind BWL Publishing Inc.,
with retired lawyer Brian Roberts.
Find more about Jude and her books here
http://bookswelove.net/authors/pittman-jude/

bookswelove.com

www.ingramcontent.com/pod-product-compliance
Lightning Source LLC
Chambersburg PA
CBHW070000120726
47909CB00003B/755